English
for International
Tourism

朗文旅游英语
中级·教师用书

Amanda Bailey

南开大学出版社
天津

Pearson Education Limited
Edinburgh Gate
Harlow
Essex CM20 2JE
England
and Associated Companies throughout the world.

www.longman.com

First published 2003

ISBN 0 582 479827

Set in 10/12pt Times New Roman

Printed in Spain by Gráficas Estella

Acknowledgements

The author would like to thank Steven Heath for his help with the internet references.

The publishers are grateful to Dorling Kindersley for their permission to reproduce copyright material on page 80.

Designed by Jennifer Coles

Contents

Introduction

Aims of the course

English for International Tourism Intermediate is designed for people who need to improve their English because they are training to work or are already working in hotel or tourism industries. The course is intended for students who already have a basic knowledge of English. It is suitable for students studying in either a monolingual or multilingual classroom situation.

The syllabus is multi-layered. Based on topic areas and professional skills relevant to the students, it also incorporates a related comprehensive grammar and vocabulary syllabus and systematic work on speaking, listening, reading and writing. It takes an integrated approach to pronunciation and includes revision.

Structure of the course

The course consists of Students' Book, Teacher's Book, Workbook and class cassette / CD. The Students' Book contains 15 units. Each unit deals with an area of the hotel and tourism industry and related professional skills such as dealing with complaints, talking on the telephone, recommending sights and taking orders in a restaurant. In addition, each unit has a grammar and a lexical focus. After every four units there is a consolidation unit which can either be used for assessment of student progress or revision. A summary of the unit contents can be found on pages 4–5 of the Students' Book.

The notes in the Teacher's Book are designed to help teachers use the material in the Students' Book most effectively and adapt it in terms of procedure, length or difficulty to suit their own classes. It includes explanations of terminology and references specific to the hotel and tourism industries for teachers not familiar with the subject. There is also a bank of photocopiable materials on pages 77–88 of the Teacher's Book which can be used to extend or adapt a lesson, or for revision later.

Skills

The four skills – reading, writing, listening and speaking – are practised and developed in each unit of the Students' Book. The teaching material comes from a wide range of sources related to the hotel and tourism industry, including the *Dorling Kindersley Eyewitness Travel Guides* (see later), travel and tourism-related websites, travel brochures and journals and so on. The varied tasks in each unit are suited to the needs of hotel and tourism students, providing many opportunities for students to use their existing knowledge of the English language and the new input in a wide range of contexts relevant to their field.

The range of text types throughout the Students' Book reflect the industry and provide the students with practice in different real-life situations from writing letters of apology and CVs to dealing with customers on the telephone, taking orders in a restaurant and giving presentations.

Listening: There are listening tasks in each unit. The listening extracts, which are on both cassette and CD, are again relevant to the industry, including dialogues between hotel staff and guests, between travel agents and customers and a tour guide explaining about a museum and its exhibits. The tapescripts for each extract are provided at the end of the Students' Book on pages 130–144 and can be used to give extra support for weaker listeners. They can also be used for self study, to check language and students can even listen and read the tapescript simultaneously.

Speaking: There is a strong focus on this skill throughout the course as the ability to communicate well in the hotel and tourism industry is essential. There are a variety of speaking activities in the Students' Book with extra suggestions for further speaking practice provided in the Teacher's Book. Students practice the language through realistic tasks and there is help with the appropriate language and level of professional formality that are necessary in different situations. The speaking tasks range from basic telephone dialogues to more complex problem-solving activities and formal presentations. The productive skills are further practised in the professional tasks (see page 5).

Reading: In both the Students' Book and the Teacher's Book guidance is given on how to approach a text to improve students' reading skills. The tasks vary from one unit to the next. Further reading practice, which can be set for homework, is provided in the Workbook.

Writing: In addition to accuracy and range of language used, students learn the importance of effective communication of message, style and organisation in formal and informal written documents. They are also given the opportunity to consolidate what they are learning by means of an on-going course project, the Travel guide project (see page 5).

Language

The language presented in the course is introduced and practised in context in both the Students' Book and the Workbook. The language introduced in each unit is highlighted in the Language focus boxes which appear throughout the Students' Book. The course provides a graded grammar syllabus combining language that is necessary for students at intermediate level and language which occurs frequently in the hotel and tourism industry.

Vocabulary

New vocabulary, which is topic-based and directly related to the hotel and tourism industry, is generally introduced through the source materials. Students are given the opportunity to practise the words in a variety of tasks in both the Students' Book and the Workbook. There are also tips in the Students' Book and Teacher's Book which help students organise and learn the new vocabulary.

Professional practice

The course has a strong focus on students developing professional skills and carrying out professional tasks. Each unit of the Students' Book has at least one professional task, the language and structure of which are provided in the Professional practice boxes. The tasks are either spoken, such as selling a conference venue or persuading a client to buy a package tour, or written, such as writing a hotel description or a covering letter for a CV.

Pronunciation

There is a strong focus on pronunciation throughout the course, especially on intonation and stress patterns. It is easy for non-native speakers of English to sound unintentionally rude or aggressive as a result of inappropriate pronunciation. Over the course, students are made aware of the pronunciation features which help them sound polite and enthusiastic. There are pronunciation tips and practice in the Students' Book, Workbook and Teacher's Book.

Consolidation units

These extra units are designed to offer a diagnostic for the students' language development. They focus on the grammar and vocabulary from the previous four units, reviewing them in slightly different contexts. The exercises can be used selectively throughout the course or set as a test at the end of every four units.

Weblinks

Reference is made throughout the Teacher's Book to useful weblinks. They can be used to find information in a variety of ways depending on the school facilities and students' access to the internet, e.g., students can look up information in class, students can research at home, or teachers can research different sites and then copy information for use in class. The weblinks are particularly useful for finding more information about the topics and places in each unit and for researching information to include in the Travel guide projects.

Google and *Ask Jeeves* are two search engines which provide an endless source of information. If you want to find information about any subject, just go to these search engines and ask for the information you require. They will then refer you to relevant websites. Give these weblinks to your students at the beginning of the course as it will help them when they need to research a topic during the course.

http://www.google.com
http://www.ask.com

Dorling Kindersley Eyewitness Travel Guides

The *Dorling Kindersley Eyewitness Travel Guides* are a series of illustrated travel guides which give extensive information about different destinations around the world. They provide detailed information on the history, culture and customs, sites, things to do, places to stay, places to eat and travel tips for the city / country. Many of the reading texts in the Students' Book are taken from these guides, thus providing authentic texts for class use. The guides themselves also serve as a useful reference for teachers if they need more information about the destinations in the units. These guides are the basis for the Travel guide project.

Travel guide project

As an integral part of the course, students are encouraged to write a travel guide for their own city or area. This guide is added to throughout the course and is based on the *Dorling Kindersley Eyewitness Travel Guide* features that are integrated into the Students' Book. The project can be done individually, in pairs or in small groups. It gives students the opportunity to consolidate language and vocabulary input in a personalised context. The Teacher's Book indicates when students should produce something for the project, what information they should include and how they might present the information.

Careers in tourism

Unit Notes

Exercise 1, page 6

Focus students' attention on the pictures and ask them what they can see. Students match the pictures with the sectors in pairs. Check the answers as a class. Students then discuss the questions in pairs or groups. Circulate and supply any vocabulary they need. Feed back on jobs in each sector.

1 airlines
2 car hire
3 ferry and cruise companies
4 hotels and other accommodation
5 catering

Possible answers for jobs in each sector:

- Airlines: flight attendant, check-in clerk, pilot.
- Car hire: customer service representative, rental location manager, reservations agent, travel trade manager (responsible for partner relationships with business and leisure travel agencies).
- Ferry and cruise companies: cruise director, purser (responsible for financial matters and passenger care), cabin / chief steward (looks after passengers' requirements, e.g. room service and porter duties), food and beverage manager, entertainments manager.
- Hotels and accommodation: manager, housekeeper, receptionist, concierge (deals with guests' needs and special requests, e.g. onward travel arrangements).
- Catering: waiter, chef, cook, food and beverage manager, wine waiter, sous chef, kitchen assistant, bartender.

Exercise 2, page 6

Elicit some ideas about what makes a good job. Check students understand the meaning of *stability, salary* and *commission*. Students order the ideas individually before discussing their choices with a partner.

Exercise 3, page 6

Check students understand *rep* is short for *representative*. Emphasise that the students only need to understand the gist of each job description to answer this question. Set a time limit of one minute. Students discuss the questions in pairs or groups.

Exercise 4, page 6

Before the students read the text in more detail, check the meaning of *a salary package,* (which might include a pension scheme, private health insurance, discounts for products and services offered by the company), *to handle* (to have responsibility for), *a query, a complaint, business figures, IT skills* (information technology / computer skills), *to be on the move, to deal with* (to handle), *to boost.* Students discuss the answers in pairs before checking with the whole class.

Extra Activity

Alternatively, divide the job descriptions between students, one or two each. Students check comprehension and vocabulary with others working on the same description(s). Books closed, students regroup and describe the job(s) they read about to their partner or group, explaining new vocabulary. They then discuss questions 3 and 4 together.

There may be some discussion here, depending on whether students rely on the explicit information in the job adverts or what is implied in the description.

1 B ('maximising room occupancy'), C, D
2 A, B
3 D
4 D
5 A, C
6 A ('excellent customer service skills'), C

Exercise 5, page 7

Check the meaning of *duties* (responsibilities). Encourage students to refer to the text to complete the exercise.

The following are wrong:
1 make
2 book
3 produce
4 possess
5 design
6 supervise

Extra Activity

Students discuss the duties involved in their jobs / a job they would like to do. *Are there any duties that the job involves that are not on the list?* Supply any vocabulary they need. *Which duties do they (think they would) like / not like doing and why?*

Workbook: Duties, page 4, exercise 2.

Vocabulary box, page 8

Refer students to the job descriptions and ask them to find and underline examples of the use of the word *skill*. Ask students to define *skill*:

Skill is an ability to do something well. It may be the result of training, experience or may be natural. (A natural skill can also be called a *talent*.)

Focus students' attention on the vocabulary box. Check students' comprehension by asking: *Is a skilful action one that is done very well or very badly? Does a highly-skilled chef have a lot or a little skill? Does an unskilled job need a lot or no skill?* Ask students for more examples of highly-skilled and unskilled jobs.

Workbook: Skills, page 6, exercise 6.

Exercise 6, page 8

Check students understand *a chambermaid, a schedule* (a plan of things that will happen or must be done), *a call centre* (a large office in which a company's employees provide information to its customers, or sell or advertise its goods or services by telephone). Students do the exercise individually or in pairs.

1 communication skills 2 computer / IT skills
3 unskilled 4 skilled 5 telephone skills
6 highly-skilled

Extra Activities

- Students write two or three sentences about themselves using variations on the word *skill*, e.g., *I want to improve my computer skills*, and compare with a partner.
- In pairs, students choose a different job from exercise 1 and write a job description using the model reading texts and the vocabulary of duties and skills. They then form new pairs and read their job description to their partner who guesses the job.
- Students write a job description for their job / a job they would like to do.
- Students search for tourism jobs on the internet. The following websites are useful: www.monster.com or www.jobs.co.uk. They choose one or two jobs of interest to them and make a note of the duties involved and skills required. They read their description to a partner who guesses the job.

Exercise 7, page 8

Ask students to predict which job she does. Emphasise that they only need to identify the job. In pairs, students discuss the answer and what information led them to it before checking as a whole class.

Travel sales consultant

Exercise 8, page 8

In pairs, students complete the answers they know. Play the cassette again, pausing after one or two questions have been answered. Students discuss their ideas in pairs before checking as a class. Repeat this method with the rest of the questions. This will give you the opportunity to assess their listening skills and to identify weak students. The exercise will also give you the opportunity to assess their competence in question formation.

1 She saw an advert for the job in a travel magazine which she got when she booked a holiday.
2 Answers questions on the phone from new and existing clients, deals with people who have made appointments and people off the street who have queries.
3 People who have an appointment or come in off the street.
4 People ask her about flights, prices and the weather.
5 How long do you want to go away for? How much money do you want to spend?
6 Do you travel free? What countries do you go to on holiday?
7 Malaysia and Boston (USA).

Extra Activities

• If there is anyone in the class who has work experience / works / wants to work as a travel sales consultant, ask them if they agree with this description of the job.
• At the end of the interview the interviewer says 'It sounds like a good life'. Do the students agree?

Language focus, page 9

Draw students' attention to the Language focus box. Most students should be familiar with these two types of question forms. Highlight that questions are usually formed by inverting the subject and auxiliary verb. To check comprehension, tell students that all the questions are from an interview. In pairs, students decide who asked each question, the interviewer *(I)* or the candidate *(C)*. Be prepared to explain / translate *a brochure* (a small book with pictures that gives you information about something, e.g. holiday brochure), *available* (free to start work), *to be in charge of, to let someone know* (to inform someone).

Students listen to the intonation of the questions. Ask students if it goes up or down at the end. Point out that *Yes / No* questions normally go up at the end while *How / Wh-* questions normally go down at the end.

Workbook: Asking questions, page 6, exercises 4 and 5.

Exercise 9, page 9

Students do the exercise individually or in pairs. During feedback, monitor the students' intonation.

1 What	I was a receptionist
2 What	Spanish, French and a little Arabic
3 Which	I'm most fluent in Spanish
4 What kind of	I'd like to work for an airline
5 How long	Just a week
6 Why	I like meeting people
7 When	As soon as possible
8 Whose	Mrs Young's

Exercise 10, page 9

Allow students time to think about their questions and answers. As students interview each other, circulate and supply any vocabulary they need. Encourage students to ask follow-up questions based on their partner's answer. Fast finishers can ask questions on further topics, e.g. home, family, studies, likes, dislikes. Note down correct and incorrect use of question forms for analysis and correction. Students report back on any interesting / unexpected information.

Extra Activity

If students already know each other well, students can pretend to be someone else in the class and answer the questions as if they were that person. At the end, their partner guesses who they are.

Exercise 11, page 10

Check that everyone understands what a CV is. Point out that it is called a résumé in US English. Students discuss the questions in groups or as a class before listening to the cassette. Don't worry about students not having all the details at this stage. They can listen for more detail in the second listening.

Fact File

Ideas on what makes a good CV vary from country to country. The advice here is aimed at job applicants in the UK. North European CVs tend to be factually objective. US CVs, by contrast, can be more self-promotional. Ask students what type of CV is most acceptable in their country.

1 It is divided into clear headings, includes information on topics, shows how you meet the criteria for the job and is well-presented.
2 No more than two sides of A4 paper
3 Personal information and a photo (depending on the company), your education and qualifications, professional skills and interests.

1 equivalent of British 'A' levels, specialising in economic subjects; vocational training in Leisure and Tourism
2 hotels
3 night auditor and assistant manager

Exercise 12, page 10

Check the meaning of *stationery*. In pairs, students answer the questions they know before listening again. Go through the answers with the whole class.

1 T
2 F (some employers like to see a photo)
3 T
4 F ('you don't need to use complete sentences as long as it's clear')
5 F ('an employer likes to know what kind of person you are and things like team sports, for example, show this')
6 T
7 T
8 T

Students look at the CV. Ask some simple comprehension questions, e.g. *What's his name? Where's he from? What languages does he speak?* Ask students which of the jobs on page 7 they think he is applying for (night auditor) before discussing the further questions as a class.

The CV follows the advice except he has not put the most recent qualifications and experience first. The information under these headings should ideally be dated.
The answer to the second question will depend on the nationality of your students.

Exercise 13, page 10

Students discuss the questions in pairs before checking the answers as a class. Check the meaning of *internship* (a work placement usually undertaken towards the end of a vocational training course).

Fact File

26,000 *covers p.a.* means that the hotel has the capacity to provide that many meals a year.

Writing CVs

Highlight the use of action verbs in the model CV, e.g. *supervised, dealt with, implemented, collected and compiled* (figures), *entered* (statistics), *to produce* (reports). Students use the context to work out the meaning of these verbs. Elicit / explain the effect of using these verbs. In pairs or as a class, students can then translate the other verbs in the Professional practice box on page 10.

Extra Activity
Students write about their own experiences / responsibilities using action verbs and compare them with a partner.

Workbook: Action verbs, page 64, exercise 3.

Exercise 14, page 11

This activity is best done in class time so students can work together in generating and organising ideas and improving the first draft. It should take about 45–60 minutes to reach this point. Students could then write a final draft for homework.

Explain that they are going to write a draft CV and that *a draft* is a piece of writing which will probably be changed and improved, it is not the final version.

Give students five minutes to note down what they would include in their CV. Typical notes:

work experience – tour guide with *Eurotours*, summer 2000
– travel agent in *Sunshine Holidays*, July & August 2001
address
24 years old
education – Travel and Tourism course, 2001 to present

Students then compare their notes with a partner, checking for any unnecessary / inappropriate information or obvious omissions. Together, they then organise both sets of notes in terms of layout and order in preparation for the first draft.

Set a time limit of 20 minutes for students to individually write the first draft. Remind students to use action verbs and refer them to the duties and skills vocabulary in the unit. Circulate and help with any problems.

Students then exchange their first drafts and provide spoken or written feedback based on the questions in the Students' Book. You may wish to put the following additional / more specific questions on the board:

Is the information in an appropriate order?
Is the information well-spaced on the page?
Are the headings clear?
Is the proportion of information under each heading appropriate?
Could an English speaker understand the education and qualifications references?
Is the language appropriate (uses action verbs, etc.)?
Is the grammar and spelling accurate?

Circulate and monitor the students' evaluations. It may be useful to highlight particularly good examples of language or presentation and / or general weaknesses to the whole class.

If students write a final version for homework, follow up the next class by putting students in groups to compare their CVs and decide which is the most impressive and why.

Extra Activity

Students read the job advertisement for Global Tours on page 13 and write the draft CV with this job in mind. If students have limited experience, allow them to invent information. They will then be able to use this CV in the interview at the end of the unit.

Exercise 15, page 12

Check the meaning of *a cover letter* (a letter you write enclosing something else). Check words: *to acquire, to call in*. Students organise the ideas in pairs or groups before checking as a class.

Do
- type your letter of application
- point out professional skills you have acquired
- emphasise how you believe you meet the employer's needs

Don't
- use interestingly coloured paper
- write more than two pages
- repeat what is already on your CV
- tell the employer that you will call in to discuss your application

---

Exercise 16, page 12

Students read the cover letter and say what the purpose of each paragraph is (1 = why I am writing, 2 = my current

position, 3 = former experience, 4 = how to contact me). Check the meaning of *background* (education and experience) and *convenience*. Students complete the letter in pairs or individually. Point out the conventions of a formal letter in English and refer students to the Writing bank on page 120 of the Students' Book.

Fact File

Conventions of a formal letter:
The writer's address goes in the top right-hand corner, with the date below. The name and address of the person they are writing to go below it on the left.
If you don't know the person's name, you write *Dear Sir* or *Madam* and you should finish *Yours faithfully*.
If you know the person's name you write *Dear Ms Brown* and finish *Yours sincerely*.
It is unacceptable to use contracted forms in formal letters.

---

1 I am writing with reference to
2 Please find enclosed
3 I have experience of
4 I am confident
5 I am available
6 I look forward to hearing

Extra Activity

Using the Global Tours job advert again (page 13), students write a cover letter to accompany their CV.

Workbook: Cover letters, pages 7 and 8, exercises 7 and 8.

Exercise 17, page 13

This activity should take about 45 minutes. For the interview to be successful, it needs careful preparation. This preparation is best done in class where students can assist each other with comprehension and pool ideas, although it could also be done at home.

Fact File

Racking means the arrangement of brochures on the brochure racks. If a company enjoys *guaranteed racking* its brochures will always be displayed at travel agencies.

Write the following questions on the board for students to discuss in pairs: *When was your last job interview? Did the interview go well? What advice would you give someone going for an interview?* (For students without job interview experience, concentrate on the last question.)

Tell students that they are going to role-play an interview. Students read the advert to find out what jobs are being advertised. Check words: *to seek* (want), *to recruit*. Divide students into *A*s and *B*s. (If there are an uneven number of students in the class, have an extra interviewer, *B*.) Explain that *A*s are the candidates and *B*s are the interviewers. Allow 20–30 minutes for this preparation stage.

A students
Students work together in small groups. Refer them to the appropriate page in the Students' Book. They should give their CV (and cover letter) to student *B*. Students read the 'During the interview' notes. Check words: *to lean forward / back, to back up*. Check comprehension by asking the students *How are you going to sit? What are you going to do before answering a question? What sort of questions require short / long answers?* etc. In their group, students then anticipate questions they might be asked and practise their responses, trying to provide examples from experience where appropriate. They also need to choose / prepare questions they are going to ask the interviewer.

B students
Students work together in small groups. Give them a few minutes to read the notes.

Words to check: *acquisition* (buying), *long-haul, racking* (see notes), *turnover*.

Students read the 'Interviewing procedure' notes. Be prepared to explain / translate: *to put someone at ease, small talk*. Check comprehension by asking *What do you need to do before the interview? How are you going to start the interview? How are you going to end the interview?* etc. They then read student *A*'s CV and cover letter. Next, they need to find a subject suitable for small talk and prepare questions on that candidate's experience and qualifications. They can check these with their group and together they can choose / prepare other questions that could be asked and decide on the best order. They also need to prepare what they are going to say about Global Tours.

Pair up *A* and *B* students for the interview. For a more authentic feel, have the interviewer sitting behind a table. Students role-play the entire interview from welcoming the candidate to concluding it appropriately. Each interview should take about ten minutes. Circulate and note down errors / useful language for analysis and correction later. You may also wish to note positive / negative body language and manner. *B*s report briefly on whether they would give their candidate a job and why / why not.

Extra Activities
- With mixed ability classes, ensure that the groups during the preparation stage are a combination of weak and strong students. Pair up strong students together and weaker students together for the interview. Strong students carry out the interview with books closed.
- After the feedback on language used well and errors (and manner), students repeat the activity with a different partner, trying to incorporate the suggestions and corrections. *B*s then decide which of the two people they interviewed performed better and why.

P. Photocopiable extra, see page 77
Choosing the best candidate
You will need one copy of the job advert and one candidate profile per student.

Language: job descriptions
description of candidate's experience, skills and personality

- Give each student a copy of the job advert. Make sure that they understand what the job is and what it involves.
- Divide students into three groups, *A*, *B* and *C*. Group *A* reads the interview notes for candidate A and discusses the positive and negative aspects of that candidate, group *B* does the same with candidate B, and group *C* with candidate C.
- Regroup students into threes so one *A*, one *B* and one *C* student are now working together. Each student describes their candidate and they then compare the three candidates, choosing one of the three for the job.
- Each group presents and justifies its decision to the class.

Extra Activities
- Students write a profile of an ideal candidate for this job.
- Students role-play an interview for this job. Student *A* is the interviewer and prepares some questions to ask. Student *B* is the applicant and can invent their details.

② Destinations

UNIT OBJECTIVES

Professional practice:	Preparing a short talk
Language focus:	Present simple, present continuous
Vocabulary:	Reasons for travelling
	Describing a destination

Unit Notes

Exercise 1, page 14

Focus students' attention on the pictures and ask them what they can see. Discuss the questions as a class.

> 1 business travel
> 2 adventure holidays
> 3 mass tourism / package holidays
> 4 exhibitions and trade fairs

Exercise 2, page 14

Fact File

A *fly-drive / flight-drive holiday* is an organised holiday which includes your air ticket and the use of a car.
The *ITB fair* is held in Berlin and is the largest and most important tourism trade show in the world.

Check students understand *retired, overseas, a coach*. Students work individually or in pairs to match the types of travel with the reasons. Ask students what type of tourism their city or area attracts.

Students may ask about the difference between *a holiday, a break* or *a trip*.
The difference is partly just which words they combine with, e.g. we can talk about a skiing holiday or a skiing trip, but not a skiing break.
Holiday and *break* can be used both for a period of rest from work or study, e.g. *a summer holiday* or *summer break*, and also for a period when you travel away from home.
In terms of travelling away from home, we tend to use *holiday* (*vacation* in US English) for longer periods of a week or more.
We tend to use *break* for shorter periods, e.g. a *weekend break; a city break*.
We tend to use *trip* when we are thinking of the whole visit including the time spent in a place and the journeys there and back, and when the stay is short or involves travelling a short distance, e.g. a *business trip, a day trip*.

> 1 leisure – health and fitness
> 2 leisure – education and training
> 3 business – conferences and conventions
> 4 leisure – sporting event
> 5 business – exhibitions and trade fairs
> 6 leisure – culture
> 7 business – incentive
> 8 leisure – holiday
> 9 business – professional meetings
> 10 VFR

Extra Activity

In pairs, students tell their partners which types of tourism they have experienced. *Where did they go? Why? Did they enjoy it?*

Exercise 3, page 15

Ask if anyone has visited Los Angeles. If someone has been there, ask them when they went there and if they enjoyed it. The other students could then ask him / her about the topics in the box, revising question forms. Revise briefly the question *What is / are ... like?* as students will need this. If no-one in the class has been there, students discuss the questions in pairs. Refer back to the photos at the beginning of the unit and ask *What do you think is the main type of tourism for LA?*

Los Angeles is famous for its beaches (Venice Beach, Santa Monica Beach), people (all the movie stars who live in the Beverly Hills area), culture (as mentioned in the article) and lifestyle (shopping in Rodeo Drive, the climate).

Exercise 4, page 15

Students predict the answer to the question before checking in the article. Emphasise that they only need to answer the question. They don't need to read the whole article.

Because it has more museums, artists, writers, film-makers, actors, dancers and musicians per head of population than any other US city.

Exercise 5, page 15

Students read the statements. Individually or in pairs, they decide if they are true or false and correct the false ones. Encourage students to guess new vocabulary from context: *to claim* (to say that something is true without having any proof), *a mecca* (the most important place of pilgrimage for all muslims and used here to mean a place that people want to visit because of a particular interest, in this example its culture).

1 F (There are exactly 300.)
2 T
3 F (It is on a hilltop overlooking the city.)
4 T
5 F (Three million went there in its first year.)
6 T ('It rivals Universal Studios' so it competes for the same tourists.)

Exercise 6, page 16

Ask students what they know about Hollywood. *Do they like Hollywood films? Do they have any favourites? Who are their favourite actors and actresses?*

Fact File

Students may be interested to know that Hollywood was originally established in 1887 as a Christian community, free of saloons and gambling. Ironically the movie business, with all its decadence, started moving in to the Los Angeles district in the 1910s and came to replace this utopia. For several decades the studios generated wealth and glamour, although in recent years the area has fallen into decline. Nevertheless, several landmarks recall its Golden Age. Amongst these is Hollywood Boulevard, one of the most famous streets in the world.

Focus students' attention on the illustrations and tour guide extract about Hollywood Boulevard.

Fact File

This is the first extract from the *Dorling Kindersley Eyewitness Travel Guides*. Check students understand the vocabulary in the questions: *an effigy* (a sculpture or model of a person), *a film set, a tribute* (something that shows your respect or admiration for someone). Set a time limit of a few minutes for students to read the extract and answer the questions. Tell students not to worry about unknown vocabulary at this stage. Encourage students to work out the meaning of unknown words from the context: *to stroll, a sidewalk* (US English, UK English: *pavement*), *embedded* (fixed in a substance), *memorabilia* (objects collected because they are connected with a person or event which is thought to be very interesting), *a display* (arrangement of things for people to see), *on display, a revue* (short sketch), *showmanship, to think up, publicity stunt* (something to get people's attention), *handprint, footprint*. Feed back on the answers as a class.

1 Hollywood Wax Museum
2 Ripley's Believe It or Not®!
3 Hollywood Galaxy – The Hollywood Entertainment Museum
4 El Capitan Theater
5 Hollywood Boulevard's 'Walk of Fame'
6 The courtyard of Mann's Chinese Theater

Exercise 7, page 16

Give students a few moments to consider their answer before discussing the question with their partner.

Exercise 8, page 17

Students find and underline the adjectives used in the tour guide extract about Hollywood Boulevard. In pairs, students use their knowledge and the context the words appear in to complete as many questions as possible. They can use a dictionary such as the *Longman Active Study Dictionary*, to help finish the exercise. The pronunciation of the following words may need particular attention: *live* /laɪv/ (as opposed to the pronunciation of the verb *live* /lɪv/), *life-size* /ˈlaɪfsaɪz/, *gigantic* /dʒaɪˈɡæntɪk/ and the *-ed* endings on *recorded, restricted* and *old-fashioned*. Practise the new words by repetition drilling, marking the stressed syllable on the board.

1 b 2 a 3 d 4 c 5 e

Extra Activities

- In pairs, students think of local places and events for which they could use each of these adjectives. They then change partners, tell their new partner the place or event and their partner guesses the adjectives.
- With a strong group, students discuss which of the two opposite adjectives they prefer and explain why, e.g. *I prefer 'restricted' because when I go shopping I get confused if there is a wide choice.*

Workbook: Opposites, page 10, exercise 2.

Exercise 9, page 17

Tell students they are going to hear five conversations which take place near the five places on Hollywood Boulevard. Ask students to predict what the people might say in each conversation. Play the extracts one at a time, allowing students to compare their ideas in pairs. Play the extract again if necessary. During class feedback ask students to explain what they heard which led them to the answer.

1 Mann's Chinese Theater
2 Clarion Hotel Hollywood Roosevelt
3 El Capitan Theater
4 Hollywood Wax Museum
5 Ripley's Believe It or Not®!

Extra Activity

Students role-play a travel sales consultant and a customer. The customer wants recommendations for what they can do in Los Angeles. Explain that the consultant should find out who the customer is travelling with, how long they are planning to spend in Hollywood and what their interests are. The customer should clarify these details and respond to the consultant's suggestions.

Exercise 10, page 17

Tell students that *a feature* is an important newspaper or magazine article or television programme. Each pair decides whether to choose five places from the city, a district of the city or one street. You may also wish them to specify the type of tourist their feature is going to be aimed at, e.g. young people, families, retired couples, day-trippers, etc. They discuss which five places to include and why. Circulate and supply vocabulary where necessary. Students then regroup and explain and justify their decisions to another student. The listener should comment on whether they think they have made a good

selection. Circulate and note down errors / useful language for analysis and correction later. Feed back on the most popular ideas.

Extra Activities

- Pyramid discussion. Each pair decides on the five places they would include in a feature on their city. They then join another pair and compare and justify their ideas. Give the groups five minutes to reach a consensus. Continue joining the groups until the whole class has the same five places.
- Students decide in pairs on five places. Elicit the students' ideas on the board. Students then have to choose places they think should be eliminated and why. The student who proposed that place should defend its right to be among the top five. Students vote in the end on which five should remain.

Travel guide project

Students write a similar feature to the one of Hollywood Boulevard for a city of their choice or their own city. Encourage them to use the vocabulary from exercise 8.

Language focus, page 18

If necessary translate the uses of the tenses before getting the students to do the matching activity in pairs or groups. Summarise as a class which uses are associated with the present simple and which uses are associated with the present continuous.

1 e 2 b 3 f 4 c 5 d 6 a

Students discuss the question in pairs or groups.

- *think* in sentence 1 describes a permanent state, it is referring to your opinion
- *thinking* in sentence 2 describes a temporary activity around the time of speaking
- *having lunch* is an action which could be describing an activity in progress now or a future arrangement depending on the context (other examples are *have a bath, have a sleep*)
- *has hot summers* describes a state (other examples are *have a brother, a lot of money, green eyes*)

Workbook: Present simple and present continuous, page 11, exercise 3.

Exercise 11, page 18

Check words: *to feature* (to include as an important part). Students work individually. During feedback, ask students to justify their answers in terms of the uses of the present simple and continuous.

> 1 often feature 2 is experiencing 3 varies 4 stays
> 5 costs 6 is becoming 7 flies 8 're looking
> 9 is suffering 10 attract 11 're thinking 12 has

Exercise 12, page 19

Ask students where San Diego is (southern California, down the coast from LA). Do they know what there is to do there? Students read the text to find out and then discuss their answers in pairs. Check students understand *to boom*, *high season*. They complete the text in pairs or groups. Check the answers with the whole class.

> 1 prefer 2 appeals 3 like 4 puts on 5 attracts
> 6 consider 7 live 8 leave 9 is now becoming 10 are
> opening 11 is booming

Exercise 13, page 19

Give students one minute to think about the questions before discussing their ideas in pairs. Circulate and monitor their use of the present simple and continuous. Feed back on whether students agreed with each other's opinions.

Exercise 14, page 20

Tell students that they are now going to listen to information about a different part of the world. Focus students' attention on the photos of Moscow. Students discuss what they know about Moscow in pairs or as a class. Students copy the headings into their exercise book to give them more space to take notes. Emphasise that they should only write key words under the headings.

Fact File

- The *Kremlin* is like a self-contained city in the centre of Moscow which includes numerous palaces, armouries and churches.
- A *trolleybus* is a public transport vehicle which travels along ordinary roads and is powered by electricity from a wire above the road.
- A *bliny* is a type of pancake. The traditional filling is caviar and sour cream.

Demonstrate this with the first sentence(s) of the listening. Elicit from the students the key words: *July*, *August – warmest*. Play the cassette through and then get students to compare their ideas and add any more information their partner tells them.

Climate:
- warmest in July and August
- summer – days are long, can rain a lot
- snow from November to April

Getting around:
- easy and cheap
- from airport to city centre by bus and metro or train
- best to see central area on foot
- other parts, metro is fastest, cheapest and easiest
- buses, trolleybuses and trams where no metro

Sightseeing:
- the Kremlin, Red Square and St Basil's Cathedral
- Lenin's tomb, Gorky Park

Entertainment:
- Moscow Film Festival
- Russian Winter Festival

Food and drink:
- quick snacks – sweet and savoury pies, jacket potatoes with fillings, bliny

Exercise 15, page 20

Students organise the vocabulary in pairs or groups and then add two more to each list. Be prepared to explain / translate *tram, chilly, frozen, fairground, cab.*

Climate	humid, chilly, frozen, warm Possible additions: hot, sunny, cloudy, windy
Transport	tram, coach, underground, cab Possible additions: train, bus, bicycle, car
Entertainment	nightclub, show, concert hall, fairground Possible additions: play at the theatre, firework display, discotheque, opera house

Note that transport vocabulary is often different in US and UK English.

US	UK
trolley	tram
bus	coach
cab	taxi
subway	underground

Exercise 16, page 20

In pairs, students complete the answers they know. Play the cassette again, pausing as necessary. Students compare in pairs. Replay any parts of the dialogue if students have missed anything or got something wrong.

1 five
2 a transfer
3 the Kremlin, Red Square, St Basil's Cathedral, Lenin's tomb
4 3 km
5 a fairground, an ornamental garden, river excursions in summer
6 autumn

Extra Activity

Write the following questions on the board for the students to discuss: *Would you like to visit Moscow? Why / Why not? When would you visit Moscow? Why? What would you do there? Why?*

Exercise 17, page 21

This planning stage should take about 45 minutes. It is best done in class where students can collaborate, pooling their knowledge and ideas both in terms of language and content. However, if you are short of time or have short lessons, set the note-taking stage as homework. Students can then organise and improve their talk at the beginning of the next class.

Discuss the following questions as a class:
Do you have any experience of public speaking? How did you find it? What was the most difficult part? What did you do to get over your difficulties? What do you think makes a good talk?

Some suggestions might be: clarity, delivery (chunking the speech and pausing for effect, speaking faster and slower, louder and quieter), organisation, visual material, anecdotes, humour, interesting new facts, etc.

Tell students they are going to give a short talk on a tourist destination of their choice. As a guideline each talk should last about 5–10 minutes, however this will depend on the level of the students and the size of the class. Elicit ideas for what type of information needs to be included and then check these against the planning diagram in the students' book on page 21. Students may have valid additions to the suggestions in the book, e.g. the cost of living, the location of resort, visa necessities, cultural differences (e.g. recommending women to dress modestly in Muslim countries) or current tourism developments.

Students could work individually, though it is probably best in pairs or in groups to allow more collaboration and discussion. For researching the tourist destination the following websites are useful: www.lonelyplanet.com, www.roughguides.com, www.timeout.com. Alternatively, students can use a search engine, such as yahoo.com or excite.com, to search for information on the city. Students make notes on the information. Point out that they could print off some of the photos from the site for their talk. If your students don't have access to the internet, they could use travel agents' brochures and books or you could bring in information on different cities or they could talk about their own city.

Students then read the 'preparing a presentation' points in the Students' Book. Allow five minutes for students to discuss with their partner or group what the *logical order* for their information is. There is no strict rule here, although you may wish to refer students to the tapescript for the presentation on Moscow in which the information is ordered from the macro-picture to the more detailed picture, in the order that the tourist would need / experience them:

(1) (not in Moscow presentation) General introduction: *Where is it? How many and what type of tourists does it attract?* general descriptive adjectives, e.g. cosmopolitan, historical, lively, sprawling, (2) Climate, (3) How to get from the airport to the centre, (4) Sightseeing, (5) Getting around, (6) Entertainment, (7) Food and drink.

Once students have organised their notes, draw attention to the useful phrases on page 21. Students could also go through the tapescript for the Moscow presentation on page 131 and pick out other useful phrases, e.g. *Most visitors to ... come to see ...; It's best to see ... on foot; The fastest, cheapest, easiest way to get around is ...; As far as ... is concerned; For an authentic ... experience go to ... .* It may also be worth reviewing the language of time and distance, e.g. *It's about ... kilometres from ...; It takes about ... hours by car; It's on the way to ... .* Give the students 5–10 minutes to discuss with their partner or group how and where to incorporate some of these phrases.

Students now explain their ideas to a new partner / group. Set a time limit of ten minutes, five minutes for each talk. The listener(s) should comment on any omissions, opportunities for more varied vocabulary, and grammar mistakes in the talk. Circulate and monitor.

When the content of the talk is settled, students should spend five minutes practising reading sections of it aloud to a partner to work on pausing, emphasising key ideas, intonation and pronunciation.

Extra Activity

If some students are ready before others, tell them the tourist destination of another pair / group and ask them to prepare some questions on that city that they would like answered. When they listen they can then check to see if these questions are answered and, if not, ask them at the end.

Exercise 18, page 21

If there are a large number of students in the class, divide them into groups of 6–8 so there can be two or three presentations going at a time. At the end of each presentation encourage students to ask questions. Finally, students feed back on which presentation was the most interesting, the best presented, the best illustrated, which place they would most like to visit, etc.

Extra Activities

Give the students listening to the presentation a feedback form to complete, e.g.:
What I liked about the presentation:
What could be improved:
Something new I learnt:
Question I would like to ask:

• If possible and useful for the particular needs of your students, record / video some or all of the presentations for follow-up work on areas of pronunciation and / or presentation skills.
• Students write a guide book entry for the tourist destination.

P Photocopiable extra, see pages 78–79
Choosing a place to visit

You will need both tourist information cards and two travel journalist role cards for each pair of students.

Language: present simple and continuous
place descriptions

• Put students into pairs and give one student a copy of one of the tourist information role cards and the other a copy of the travel journalist role card. Give students five minutes to read and digest the information.

• Organise the classroom so that the tourist information agent is sitting opposite the travel journalist. Students do the role-play in pairs. Point out that the travel journalist should make brief notes on things they think will interest young people.

• Students then reverse roles, using the other tourist information card and the travel journalist card.

• Students discuss which of the two places is best for the article and report their ideas back to the class.

Extra Activity

Students write up their article on the city. This can be done for homework.

---

③ Hotel facilities

Unit Notes

Exercise 1, page 22

Fact File

Some hotel publicity differentiates between room *amenities* and hotel *facilities*. You may wish to point this out to students, or simply refer to all these things as *facilities*.

Focus students' attention on the pictures and ask them to describe what they can see. Check words: *to provide* (give). In pairs, students discuss the question and make a list. Ask the pair with the longest list to feed back.

Possible answers

- Room amenities: complimentary daily newspaper, hospitality tray, hairdryer, personal safe, air conditioning, minibar, colour television, satellite channels, video player and video library, CD player and CD library, internet access, trouser press
- Hotel facilities: express check-in / check-out, 24 hour room service, laundry / dry-cleaning, currency exchange, porterage service, bar, restaurant, lounge, business centre, gift shop, beauty salon, fitness centre, sauna, jacuzzi, swimming pool, garden, car park, car valet service, car wash

Exercise 2, page 22

Ask students where you would find icons like these (in brochures and travel guides). In pairs, students match the facilities and icons. Encourage students to use a process of elimination and work out new words such as *wheelchair* and *safe*.

1 air conditioning
2 pets welcome
3 health or fitness facilities
4 wheelchair access
5 24-hour room service
6 business facilities
7 swimming pool
8 credit cards accepted
9 children's facilities
10 rooms for more than two people

Exercise 3, page 22

Give students a couple of minutes to discuss the question in pairs, before checking as a class.

1 restaurant
2 photography not allowed
3 theatre
4 cloakroom
5 tourist information
6 live entertainment
7 no smoking
8 outside eating

Workbook: Hotel facilities, page 14, exercise 1.

Exercise 4, page 22

Fact File

The Lanesborough Hotel is located on Hyde Park Corner in central London. It is rated as a five-star deluxe hotel and its 'Royal Suite' is often used by celebrities and heads of state.

Focus students' attention on the picture of the Lanesborough Hotel. Ask students *Do you think it is a basic or a luxury hotel? What kind of facilities do you think it has? How much do you think it costs per night?* Set a time limit of two minutes for students to read and make a list of the facilities. Emphasise that they are only looking for facilities at this point and should not worry about understanding everything. Feed back as a class. Check students have understood *butler* (person who attends to the needs of the guest) in this context.

- chauffeured Rolls-Royce
- butlers who find anything you want
- personalised business cards and stationery
- complimentary flowers, bottle of champagne and bowl of fruit
- fitness studio (the equipment can be moved into your room)
- in-room computer with fast internet access and internet radio
- 15 phone handsets and a mobile

Exercise 5, page 22

Students read the article again to answer the questions. They compare their ideas in pairs before feedback.

1 F (He filmed there.)
2 F (It doesn't include breakfast.)
3 T
4 F (The equipment from the fitness studio can be moved into the room.)
5 T
6 T
7 T
8 F (The film appeared 'as if by magic' in the morning.)

Exercise 6, page 23

Students match the words they already know and then find the others in the article and use the context to work out the meaning. The pronunciation of the following words may need particular attention: chauffeur /ˈʃəʊfə/, façade /fəˈsɑːd/, mobile /ˈməʊbaɪl/. Write the phonemics for these words on the board, marking the stress, and drill them chorally.

1 b 2 e 3 f 4 c 5 a 6 d 7 g

Extra Activity
- Ask students *What most impressed the writer of the article? What do you think is the most impressive facility offered by the hotel? What facilities do you look for in a hotel when you go on holiday?*
- Students read more about the hotel on its website, www.lanesborough.com. In groups, students could write five questions about the hotel that they would like to know the answers to and search on the site for the answers. Alternatively, they could use the site to write five comprehension questions for another group.

Exercise 7, page 24

Focus students' attention on the leaflet. Ask students where they would find this (in the hotel room). Give them a couple of minutes to read the information about the services. Encourage students to guess the meaning of new words from context: *dry-cleaning, a chambermaid, the person on duty, on request, to have your nails manicured.* Play the recording, pausing after each conversation for students to compare what they have understood. Replay sections if necessary.

1 beauty salon and hairdresser
2 room service (meals)
3 valet parking
4 valet service
5 business facilities

Extra Activity
With a more confident group, repeat each section, asking the students *What exactly does each guest ask for? Can the hotel provide this service?*

Language focus: Have / Get something done

Go through the language focus box as a class. Refer students to the examples and ask concept questions to check comprehension, e.g., *Does the guest want to take the sandwiches to the room himself? Does the guest want to translate the document himself? Is the speaker going to carry the bags?*

Point out the structure of the sentences:

have / get + object + past participle

get + object + infinitive

With a monolingual class, translate the sentences and compare how they are formed in English with how they are formed in the local language.

Elicit what you can have done for you at the Paragon Hotel, e.g., get someone to book theatre or concert tickets, have / get your clothing washed / dry-cleaned. Give students a couple of minutes to consider further questions before discussing with a partner. For feedback, go round the class asking each student to give an example of what you can have done for you at a luxury hotel. The winner is the student who comes up with the last idea!

Extra Activity
With less confident students, set the first question as a written task so that students can practise manipulating the form slowly, before producing it more spontaneously when discussing the second question.

Workbook: Have/Get something done, page 15, exercise 3.

Exercise 8, page 24

Tell students they are going to look at some hotels in Berlin featured in the *Dorling Kindersley Eyewitness Travel Guide*. Ask *Has anyone been to Berlin? What do you know about Berlin? What is it like?* Check students understand the vocabulary in the question: *a charge* (the price you must pay), *to ensure* (make certain). Give students two minutes to complete the exercise. Students compare in pairs before checking the answers as a class.

> 1 DeragHotel Grosser Kurfürst
> 2 Berlin Hilton
> 3 Hotel Adlon
> 4 Hackescher Markt
> 5 Four Seasons Hotel

Exercise 9, page 25

Point out that all the words are in the hotel descriptions. Students work in pairs or individually before checking answers as a class.

> **1** b **2** e **3** d **4** a **5** g **6** c **7** f

Extra Activity

Quick memory test. Ask students to recall, without looking at the texts, what was described as *opulent*, *elegant*, etc. This will usefully reinforce words that commonly go together.

Workbook: Adjectives, page 14, exercise 2.

Exercise 10, page 25

Students predict the stressed syllable before listening to check. Chorally and individually drill any words that the students have difficulty pronouncing.

> ■ bright
> ■□ stunning, charming
> ■□□ opulent
> □■□□ impeccable, spectacular, luxurious

Extra Activity

In pairs, students think of local sites and attractions for each of the adjectives. Do the first one together as a class. Students then change partners and see if they agree with each other.

Exercise 11, page 25

Students ask and answer the question in pairs. Encourage them to refer to the picture and the map as well as the description. This speaking activity may provide an opportunity for you to assess the students' competence with the language of making comparisons.

Travel guide project

Students design and write the text for a feature on the best hotels in their city / area. They could look up further information on hotels in their area on the internet, either using the name of a hotel or using a search engine, such as yahoo.com or excite.com, and 'hotels in (name of city / area)'. Encourage them to use the vocabulary from exercise 9.

Language focus, page 26

Students read the examples and use them to complete the rules. Draw attention to the language tip on *than*. You may also wish to highlight the /ə/ sounds in the four examples:

more expensive th*a*n, thən

th*e* busiest, thə

old*er* thən, oldər thən

*a*s expensive *a*s, əs expensive əs

Test students' comprehension by writing some more adjectives on the board, e.g. *cheap, big, famous, attractive, noisy, dirty,* and ask students to use the rules to form the comparative and superlative. Use these to highlight the spelling changes for one-syllable adjectives: if an adjective ends in one vowel + one consonant, double the consonant. Go through the irregular forms.

> **1** a **2** c **3** b **4** d

Workbook: Making comparisons, page 15, exercise 4.

Exercise 12, page 26

Give students a couple of minutes to study the information on the four hotels taken from the *Dorling Kindersley Eyewitness Travel Guide for Berlin*. In pairs, students complete the text. Monitor and help where necessary. Be prepared to explain / translate: *to mind (sharing)* (to feel unhappy about), *to be worth the higher price* (good idea despite higher price), *to cater for someone* (to provide what they need or want). Feed back by getting students to read the text aloud. Monitor their pronunciation. Ask students which hotel they would choose and why.

1   the largest
2   the most comfortable
3   the cheapest
4   more expensive than
5   higher
6   the same as
7   easier
8   quieter (although *quiet* is a two-syllable adjective, the comparative and superlative are usually formed by adding *-er* and *-est*)
9   as well-equipped as
10 the most suitable

Extra Activity
With stronger students, encourage them to compare the hotels orally before reading and completing the text.

Exercise 13, page 27
Refer students to the appropriate pages and give them a couple of minutes to study the information. With a less confident group, get the students to prepare the questions they need to ask in pairs. Put *A* and *B* students together and allow five minutes for them to complete the tables. Students remain in their pairs and orally compare the six hotels. Encourage them to use the adjectives from exercise 13. Circulate and monitor, concentrating on the use of comparatives and superlatives. Note down errors / useful language. Feed back briefly on which hotel they would prefer to stay in and why, before analysing / correcting the language points.

Tip: During an information gap activity, make sure that students cannot read their partner's information. One way to do this is to have the students sitting at a distance from each other. This has the added advantage of making monitoring easier.

Extra Activity
- Guessing game. Students work in pairs. Student *A* chooses one of the six hotels and describes it by comparing it to two or three other hotels. Student *B* listens and, at the end, identifies the hotel. Do an example of your own with the class first.
- Students write a section for a hotel guide, similar to the one in exercise 12, based on these six hotels.
- Students research three or four local hotels. Use a search engine, such as yahoo.com or excite.com, and search for 'hotels in (name of city)'. They present their information to a partner, comparing and contrasting the hotels and saying what type of traveller they would be most suitable for. The listener decides which one they would stay in and why.

Exercise 14, page 27
Give students 2–3 minutes to consider what they can say about each of the topics. Circulate and monitor the discussion.

Extra Activity
With a less confident group you may wish to elicit adjectives which could be used, e.g. *wide* (range / variety of), *modern, clean, helpful, friendly, useful, fast*.

P Photocopiable extra, see pages 80–81
Choosing a hotel
You will need one copy of the tourist information role card and one tourist role card for each pair of students.

Language: making comparisons
              describing hotels

- Put students into pairs and give one student a copy of the tourist information role card and the other a copy of the tourist role card. Give students a couple of minutes to read and understand the information.

- Organise the classroom so that the tourist information agent sits behind a desk, facing the tourist. Point out that the tourist should decide which hotel they are going to book. Students do the role-play in pairs.

Students report as a class on which hotel was chosen and why.

Exercise 15, page 28

Students discuss the questions in pairs or open class. For a more guided speaking exercise, students could predict the answers to exercise 16.

Exercise 16, page 28

Set a time limit of three minutes for students to read the article and complete the table. Emphasise that they should scan the article for the relevant information and that they should try to work out the meaning of unknown words from the context. Students compare in pairs before checking the answers as a class. Check students have understood: *a gratuity* (formal for *a tip*), *a food trolley*, *dusty curtains, a pillow, a towel*.

area	checks
concierge	provides a full service and not expect a tip
restaurant	quality of service without tipping
room service	staff are helpful in suggesting what to order, food trolley is clean
bedroom	under the bed, curtains, minibar, pillows
bathroom	towels, instant water, easy to use shower, no hairs in bath

Exercise 17, page 29

Allow students a further five minutes to read the article in more detail and find the answers to the questions. Students discuss their answers in pairs before feeding back as a class.

1 To ensure standards are maintained, so hotel can justify higher rates.
2 No, the stay is anonymous.
3 It goes on a six-month trial at the end of which is a second hotel inspection. If it fails this test it loses its 'Preferred Hotels' status.
4 In the USA and Asia.
5 Assuming that he stays in a different hotel every night, he inspects 144 hotels a year.
6 Because they shouldn't expect a tip and it shouldn't affect the quality of service.

Extra Activity

Write the following questions on the board for students to discuss: *What are the advantages and disadvantages of working as a hotel inspector? Would you like to work as a hotel inspector?*

Exercise 18, page 29

Students study the inspection form. Check words: *lobby* (reception area), *carpet, tidiness, hygiene, appliances* (piece of equipment), *fittings* (the things that are fixed in a building), *linen* (sheets, tablecloths, etc.), *tableware* (knives, forks, spoons, plates, glasses, etc.). Ask students to discuss what circumstances would lead to the area being marked as 'poor'. Monitor and supply vocabulary. This should give you the opportunity to pre-teach some of the vocabulary from the listening activity, e.g. *faded in the sunlight, worn, cracked, stained*. Play the recording, pausing after each area for students to compare what they have understood. Replay any sections that students are unsure about. Feed back on which sections are marked as 'poor'.

The following are all poor:
• Front entrance – signs & notices
• Lobby – carpets, tidiness, service
• Kitchen – hygiene, food storage
• Restaurant – linen, tableware
• Bathrooms – fittings
• Bedrooms – fittings, TV / handsets

Extra Activity

With a stronger class, get students to identify exactly what the faults are on the second listening.

Exercise 19, page 29

Students read the introduction on page 29. Check words: *refurbish* (to make something look new and bright again). Ask students *What are the two things that you have to decide?* (what they are going to do and how they are going to advertise it).

Refer students to the price list on page 109 of the Students' Book. Check words: *utensils, roof, fridge, freezer, passageway, oak furniture*.

Give students a few minutes to think about the problem individually and make a note of their ideas. This means that they have considered the problem before discussing it and helps avoid the situation where one student dominates.

Organise the students in groups of 3–4 for the discussion. Set a time limit of ten minutes for groups to make and record their decisions. Circulate and monitor, making a note of useful language / errors for analysis and correction later.

Feed back briefly on their decisions.

Exercise 20, page 29

Depending on whether your students have access to authentic examples, this activity should take 20–30 minutes. Most hotel descriptions in travel guides are about four or five sentences long and use a lot of positive adjectives, like those in exercise 9. Students work together in small groups. Give them five minutes to decide what features of the hotel and adjectives they want to include in the description.

If possible, students then look at some examples of authentic travel guide descriptions. These can be found at travel guide sites, e.g., www.lonelyplanet.com, www.roughguides.com. Allow students 5–10 minutes to look through these for useful expressions and vocabulary. They could use a monolingual dictionary to check unknown words.

Finally, set a limit of five minutes for students to write the final copy. Students read other groups' descriptions and vote on the most effective.

④ Tour operators

Unit Notes

Fact File

The theme of this unit is *tour operators*. Tour operators are companies which put together all the component parts of a holiday, e.g. the means of travel, accommodation, facilities, transfers, excursions, and sell them as a package, usually through a travel agent though sometimes directly to the customer.

Exercise 1, page 30

Students look at the pictures and describe what they can see. What decades do they think the pictures show? Students discuss the questions in pairs or small groups.

1 adventure holidays
2 seaside holidays
3 cruise holidays
4 flying abroad

Exercise 2, page 30

Students read the statements first. Check the meaning of *demanding* (expects very high standards), *profits, prevent.* Set a time limit of two minutes for students to read the extracts and match the names and opinions. Ask students to underline the sentences in the extracts which led them to the answer. Encourage students to guess the meaning of new words from context. Students compare answers in pairs before checking with the class.

Pile them high, sell them cheap refers to the policy of selling a lot of travel products at relatively cheap prices.

1 Noel Josephides
2 Simon Laxton, Mike Gooley
3 Roger Shaw
4 Noel Josephides, Simon Laxton
5 Simon Laxton, Mike Gooley
6 Simon Laxton
7 Roger Shaw

Fact File

In pairs, students discuss whether they agree or disagree with each of the statements and why.

Exercise 3, page 30

In pairs, students use their knowledge and the context the words appear in to complete as much as possible. They can use a dictionary, preferably monolingual, to help finish the exercise. Practise the new words by repetition drilling, marking the stressed syllable on the board.

1 b 2 d 3 g 4 h 5 a 6 c 7 f 8 e

Workbook: Tour operators, page 20, exercise 3.

Exercise 4, page 31

This exercise provides the opportunity both to review comparatives and superlatives from Unit 3 and to assess students' competence with the present perfect. Check students understand *booking procedure.* Give students a few minutes to think about / prepare what they are going to say. Students discuss the questions in pairs or small groups. Feed back briefly on whether students think that these changes are generally positive or negative.

Language focus, page 32

1 Draw students' attention to the Language focus box. Encourage students to use the example sentences to help complete the rules. During feedback, ask students which sentences illustrate each use. It may be useful to draw timelines on the board to help students to understand the differences, as follows:

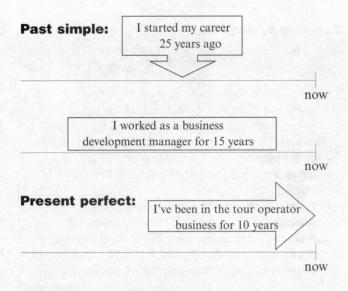

Past simple:

I started my career 25 years ago

now

I worked as a business development manager for 15 years

now

Present perfect:

I've been in the tour operator business for 10 years

now

a present perfect
b present perfect
c present perfect
d past simple
e both the present perfect and the past simple
f past simple

Extra Activity

As well as checking meaning, it may be necessary to check form. In particular, highlight the following points:

- the present perfect is formed with *have / has* + past participle
- *have* and *has* are often shortened to 've and 's
- regular past participles are verb + *-ed*, irregular ones have to be learnt individually
- in questions *have / has* and the subject are inverted
- negatives are formed with *haven't / hasn't*

Workbook: Present perfect and past simple, pages 21 and 22, exercises 4 and 5.

2 Check the students understand the meaning of *so far* (up to now). In pairs, students copy the time expressions into two columns: those used with the past and those used with the present perfect. Encourage students to refer back to the uses of the two tenses to help. Feed back as a class. Elicit some more examples from students, e.g. past simple: *five minutes ago, last summer*, present perfect: *recently, over the last few months*.

- Used with the past: *yesterday, last week, six months ago, in 2002*
- Used with the present perfect: *lately, so far, over the last few years, since* + point in time

---

Extra Activity

Ask students questions beginning: *How long have ...* (you lived in your present house)? *How long did ...* (your journey to college take this morning)? *When did you ...* (last go to the cinema)? Students only write down the time expressions in answer to each question. At the end, students look at the time expressions they have written down, reconstruct the question and ask their partner. Encourage students to ask follow-up questions, too.

Exercise 5, page 32

Students work individually before comparing in pairs. Encourage students to resolve any differences with their partner by justifying their answers.

1 organised **2** wasn't **3** has worked **4** did you start
5 have become **6** has fallen **7** 've had **8** have increased
9 started **10** have put

Exercise 6, page 33

Focus students' attention on the magazine article and ask students if they know anything about Airtours or MyTravel. Students read the article quickly and then tell their partner what they have learnt about Airtours and MyTravel. Check the meaning of *chain of outlets* (a group of travel agencies), *to acquire, a brand* (the name of a well-known product made by a particular company). Students complete the profile individually or in pairs.

1 grew **2** created **3** sold **4** was **5** began
6 continued **7** announced **8** has become
9 has been **10** has enabled **11** have tripled

Extra Activity

- Students write a profile of the company they work for, using the past simple and present perfect.
- Students research a company on the internet and write a profile of it for a trade magazine. Many travel companies include a company history on their website. Students can find them by using a search engine, such as yahoo.com or excite.com, looking for 'travel companies' and then looking up individual companies.

Exercise 7, page 33

Drill the pronunciation of the three sounds. Students could predict the pronunciation of the words in the box before listening to the cassette to confirm their ideas. When students feed back their answers, check for accurate pronunciation.

- /ɪ/ *live, business, holiday, tourism, service*
- /iː/ *leave, opportunities, industry, money*
- /aɪ/ *exciting, environment, high*

Extra Activity
Students find more examples of words containing these sounds in the text, e.g. /ɪ/ *division, biggest*, /iː/ *employees, e-commerce*, /aɪ/ *airline, worldwide*.

Workbook: /ɪ/ ,/iː/, /aɪ/ sounds, page 21, exercise 3.

Exercise 8, page 34

- Students often have difficulties with the difference between *he's been to* and *he's gone to*. You may wish to clarify this at the beginning of the exercise. Both of these words are used as past participles of *to go* but with different meanings: *he's been* means that he has 'travelled to and returned from', *he's gone* means that he has 'left for' (he is on his way there) or 'travelled to' (hasn't returned).

When talking about experiences the present perfect is used to start the topic, e.g. *Have you been to Canada? I've been to France once.* The follow-up questions and answers are generally in the past, as you are then referring to a specific completed past event.

Ask students to think about cities they have visited. Demonstrate the activity with a group of three. With a less confident class, elicit and write up the question sequence: *Have you ever been to … ? When did you go there? Who did you go with?* Highlight the weak pronunciation of *been* /bɪn/. Draw attention to the change from present perfect to past. Encourage students to show interest in their partners' answers by asking follow-up questions. Monitor and correct where necessary.

Extra Activity
- Follow-up game. One group reports back their information, e.g. *Two of us have been to Rome.* The other students in the class then have two minutes to question members of that group on their visit to Rome, e.g. *What did you see there? What was the weather like?*
- All members of the group pretend to have visited Rome. The rest of the class have two minutes to ask as many questions as possible about their visits to Rome. At the end of two minutes the class must guess who has really been there.

Exercise 9, page 34

Fact File
- A *scheduled flight* is one that operates to a published timetable, on defined routes and under government licence. It runs regardless of the number of passengers and is therefore used mainly by business travellers who are prepared to pay a higher price for the convenience and flexibility offered.
- *Charter flights* evolved in response to the growing package holiday industry. They are generally cheaper as operators aim to fill as many seats as possible, often only offering the flight if they can be guaranteed a minimum number of passengers.

Tell students that *ancillary services* are extra / additional services. Check the meaning and pronunciation of new words, encouraging students to teach each other instead of / before providing the answer yourself. Practise the new words by repetition drilling, marking the stress on the board. Students organise the vocabulary in pairs or groups. Briefly discuss with the students the value of recording vocabulary in web diagrams. Point out that:

- the process of organising words by meaning makes the words more memorable
- you can return to the word diagram and add new words in the future

- A *guesthouse* is a small cheap hotel.
- An *inn* is a pub where you can stay the night, usually in the countryside.
- A *lodge* is a house typically used by people who do countryside sports, e.g. ski / hunting lodge.
- A *villa* is a house usually in the countryside or near the sea, particularly in southern Europe.

- Types of holiday: cruise, adventure, mini-break, honeymoon, winter sports, all-inclusive
- Accommodation: hotel, guesthouse, lodge, villa, inn
- Transportation: charter flight, scheduled flight, luxury coach
- Ancillary services: visa, transfer, foreign exchange, equipment hire, insurance, lift pass

Extra Activity
- In pairs, students discuss which type of holiday, transportation and accommodation they prefer and why.
- Students add two more to each category.

Workbook: Package holidays, page 22, exercise 6 and page 68, exercise 11.

Exercise 10, page 34

Check students understand *a complaint, to complain.* Ask students if they have ever had any bad holiday experiences. *Did they complain? Who to? What was the response?* Elicit one or two common complaints about package holidays before putting the students in pairs to discuss the question. They could write a list, in which case ask the pair with the longest list to feed back.

Exercise 11, page 34

Set a time limit of a few minutes for students to read the email on page 35 of the Students' Book and make a list of the complaints. Check words: *to lack, dawn.* Fast finishers discuss which issue they think is the most serious.

- *outward flight was delayed*
- *check-in staff were unhelpful*
- *there was no representative from Med Tours*
- *food in hotel lacked variety and service was poor*
- *beach was across a busy main road and at least 20 minutes' walk away*
- *shops in the resort were crowded and expensive*
- *noisy roadworks in town*
- *had to leave resort at dawn to get to airport in time for return flight: the stay is not seven days.*

Exercise 12, page 34

Check the meaning of *to raise an issue* (to introduce a point), *compensation* (money given to someone because of inconvenience / injury caused by someone else). Students discuss the questions in pairs or groups before checking with the class.

- *At the airport, the tour operator should keep their clients fully and regularly updated and provide refreshments depending on the length of the delay. If there is not a tour operator representative at the airport, one from the airline should be made available and clients informed at check-in who to see.*
- *Hotel service is the responsibility of the hotel.*
- *Hotel advertised as 'a stone's throw from the beach' – the tour operator is responsible for the accuracy of its brochures.*
- *In reference to shops, brochure should state something like 'lively resort'.*

- *Roadworks <u>next to the hotel</u> must be notified before departure and, if severe, the client given the option to change hotels or cancel at no charge.*
- *A seven-day holiday counts as a room being available to the client over seven nights, if this was the case the client does not have a case.*
Genuine case for compensation:
- <u>*Beach was across a busy main road and at least 20 minutes' walk away.*</u>

Exercise 13, page 35

The planning stage of this writing activity is best done in class so students can work together in generating and organising their ideas. It should take about 30 minutes to reach this stage. Students could write the final version for homework.

Write the following questions on the board for students to discuss in pairs: *What are the objectives of replying to a letter of complaint?* (Pacify the customer, provide an explanation, say what action will be taken, offer some compensation) *What 'tone' is appropriate to achieve these objectives?* (Apologetic, grateful for bringing problems to their attention, efficient). *What types of action can a tour operator take in response to a complaint?* (Explain the cause of the problem, correct the brochure, pass on the complaint to the relevant manager, give the customer a discount off a future holiday, refund the customer a part of what he / she paid). Feed back as a class.

In pairs, students look at Mr Grundy's complaints from exercise 11 and make a note of which points they are going to respond to and how they are going to respond to each. Set a time limit of ten minutes.

Refer students to the Professional practice box 'Letters of apology'. Check the students understand *bring this matter to our attention* (tell us about this situation), *be assured.* Give students a further ten minutes to organise their ideas into paragraphs, identifying where they could use some of the expressions. Refer students to page 120 of the Writing Bank in the Students' Book.

Students then explain their draft to another pair. Write the following questions on the board for the listeners to comment on:

Will the customer be satisfied with this reply?
Are the explanations / actions taken appropriate?
Is the letter well-organised, with clear paragraphs?
Does the letter follow the conventions of formal letter writing?
Is the grammar and spelling accurate?

Circulate and monitor the students' evaluations. It may be useful to highlight particularly good examples of language or organisation and / or general weaknesses to the class.

Students could write the final copy in class or for homework. You may wish to show students this suggested answer to compare with their letters.

Sample answer:

Med Tours
106 Netherwood Rd
London W14 3PG

Mr Arthur Grundy
7 St Luke's Rd
Tunbridge Wells
TN4 9CG

Dear Mr Grundy

Thank you for your letter regarding your recent holiday with Med Tours. We are very sorry to hear that you were dissatisfied with the organisation of the holiday, as we try to ensure that all our customers receive a high quality service.

In your letter you mentioned several inconsistencies between the brochure and the conditions in the hotel, particularly the distance from the beach and the length of the stay. Thank you for bringing this to our attention. Be assured that we will amend the information in the brochure.

We were sorry to hear that the staff were unhelpful during your delay at the airport. It is company policy that clients who are delayed are kept fully updated and provided with refreshments and we will look into why this did not occur.

The further inconveniences you suffered relating to the hotel and the resort, while not our direct responsibility, are of concern to us and we will investigate them.

We value your custom and, as compensation for the inconvenience you have suffered, we would like to offer you a 30% discount on your next holiday with Med Tours.

Once again, our sincerest apologies for the inconvenience caused and we look forward to hearing from you.

Yours sincerely

James Greenwald

Manager

Extra Activity
- Students role-play a telephone conversation between Mr Grundy and a representative of Med Tours. Mr Grundy explains his complaints and the compensation he would like. The representative is apologetic but can only offer limited compensation.
- Case studies of further 'holidays from hell' can be found at www.holidaytravelwatch.co.uk and make interesting reading material! Give students different stories to read at home and summarise at the beginning of the next class.

Workbook: Letter of apology, page 23, exercise 7.

Exercise 14, page 36

Ask students to read the brochure and decide who they think this holiday might appeal to (nationality, age, families) and why. Be prepared to explain *short / long haul* (distance). Students listen to the cassette straight through and mark the changes. With a less confident class, pause after each change and allow students to compare their ideas.

- The long stretch of sandy beach is just 100 metres away across a main road.
- The holiday includes daily sports and activities including tennis, table tennis, volleyball, mini golf, football and keep fit.
- There is an extra charge for the sauna, Turkish bath and jacuzzi.
- The price per person for departures on / between 25/06–08/07 for 14 nights is £699.

Exercise 15, page 36

In pairs, students complete the answers they know. Play the cassette again, pausing as necessary. Students compare in pairs. Replay any parts of the dialogue if students have missed anything or got something wrong.

1 right outside the hotel
2 the busy road you have to cross to get to the beach
3 because the exchange rate value of the pound has been high
4 it would look more attractive to customers

Exercise 16, page 37

This activity should take about 30 minutes. Students read the introduction. Check words: *customer resistance, poor reputation, entirely, a welcome* (useful, valued) *addition*. Ask students which is the first email and which is the response. Point out that students should read the emails in that order. Give students one minute to read the emails and find out: *When are Jane Wilkins and Michael King meeting? Are they optimistic or pessimistic about doing business together in the future? Why?*

Tell the students that they are going to role-play the meeting between Jane Wilkins of Renaissance Holidays and Michael King. Divide students into *A*s and *B*s. Explain that *A*s are Jane Wilkins, or a colleague of hers at Renaissance Holidays and *B*s are Michael King. Give the students at least ten minutes to prepare for the meeting as it is important that they feel certain and confident of their role.

A students

Students work in pairs. Refer them to page 109 of the Students' Book. Allow students five minutes to read the information and check any words with their partners / in a dictionary. Be prepared to explain / translate *good value for money* (you feel that what is offered is good in comparison with the money you pay).

B students

Students work together in pairs. Allow students five minutes to read the information and check any words with their partners / in a dictionary. Ask students to think about how they are going to start the conversation and under what circumstances they would renew the contract with Renaissance Holidays.

Revise formal greetings and elicit how the conversation might start, e.g.:

'How do you do? I'm Michael King.'

'How do you do? I'm ...'

'Please, take a seat. I understand that you would like us to renew our contract with Renaissance Holidays, however, in the past, we had a number of problems with the company. Firstly, ...'

Explain that the meeting must have a conclusion. Discuss possible conclusions with the students, e.g. *the travel agency renews the contract / it doesn't renew the contract / it agrees to a trial period / it sends one of its staff on a free Renaissance Holiday to investigate it,* etc. Pair up *A* and *B* students for the meeting. For a more authentic feel, organise the room so that Michael King can sit behind a table, with the representative facing him. Circulate and note down errors / useful language for analysis and correction later. Get pairs to feed back briefly on the outcome of their meeting.

Extra Activity

- You may wish to highlight that student *A* is talking about changes in the past with present consequences and therefore all these sentences will be in the present perfect, e.g. *We have opened up new destinations.*
- With a mixed ability class, pair up strong students together and weak students together for the meeting. Strong students could hold the meeting without referring to the notes.
- After the feedback on language used well and errors, students repeat the activity with a different partner, trying to incorporate the language suggestions and corrections.

P **Photocopiable extra, see pages 82–83**

A nightmare holiday

You will need one copy of the advertisement per student, one tourist role card and one tour operator role card for each pair of students.

Language: package holidays
complaints

- Give each student a copy of the holiday advertisement and ask them to decide which three things about the holiday are the best. Discuss the answers with the class.

- Give one half of the class the tourist role cards, and the other the tour operator role cards. Allow the students five minutes to prepare.

- Arrange the class so that each tourist is next to a tour operator. Students do the role-play in pairs. Encourage students to use the useful expressions on their role card where appropriate.

- Students report to the class on what compensation the tourist and the tour operator agreed on.

Consolidation 1

These exercises are designed to evaluate students' progress in assimilating the grammar and vocabulary from units 1–4. They are suitable for either revision or testing.

For revision purposes, review the language area with the students in open class first, and then allow the students to work together in completing the exercises. Feed back as a class, asking for justification of the answer where appropriate.

For testing purposes, set a time limit for students to do one or more of the exercises individually in class. Alternatively, set the exercises as homework. If you choose to use these exercises for testing, it is worth first discussing with the students the best approach to each exercise, in particular reading a text to understand its overall meaning before attempting to complete the gaps. Take the answers in to correct or provide the students with the answers to correct each other's.

You may also wish to evaluate students' progress in communicative performance. To do this, repeat one of the speaking / writing activities from the first four units. To increase the interest and challenge factors in this, change one or two features, e.g., students role-play an interview for a different job.

Exercise 1, page 38

Review typical questions asked in an interview. Refer to the Language focus on page 9 of the Students' Book and the Grammar reference section on page 124.

1 Where are you from?
2 How did you find out about the job?
3 What's your current job?
4 Where did you live before?
5 How often do you go back there?
6 What kind of job are you looking for?
7 Do you speak any other languages?
8 When would you like to start work?

Exercise 2, page 38

Review the uses of the present simple and present continuous and elicit examples for each. Refer to the Language focus on page 18 of the students' book and the Grammar reference section on page 124.

1 overlooks
2 Are you thinking
3 charge
4 're renovating
5 doesn't include
6 're opening, think
7 is leaving

Exercise 3, page 38

Review the rules for comparatives and superlatives. Ask students what they remember / know about Berlin. Students read the whole text and say what topics it talks about (traffic, hotels, museums, nightclubbing). Students then complete the text with the appropriate form of the words in the box. Refer to the Language focus on page 26 of the Students' Book and the Grammar reference section on page 125.

1 the busiest
2 easier
3 the same as
4 the latest
5 the finest
6 as interested

Exercise 4, page 39

Review the uses of the past simple and present perfect. Students read the letter and answer *Who is it to? Who is it from? What is the purpose of the letter?* Students then complete the exercise. Refer to the Language focus on page 32 of the Students' Book and the Grammar reference section on page 125.

1   visited
2   sent
3   needed
4   were
5   didn't work
6   have now received
7   have taken
8   have also redecorated
9   has been
10 rang

Exercise 5, page 39

Check students understand all the words. Provide an example for each stress pattern, e.g.,

□■□   attractive /əˈtræktɪv/

■□□   wonderful /ˈwʌndəfəl/

□■□□   luxurious /lʌgˈzjʊəriəs/

□■□	outgoing, resourceful, ambitious
■□□	trustworthy, confident, sociable
□■□□	dependable, professional

Exercise 6, page 39

You could set this as a race. Do the first one or two together, so students understand what they have to do.

a accommodation
b butler
c catering
d downtown
e entertainment
f facilities
g gratuity
h honeymoon
i itinerary
j journey
k kitchen
l luxurious
m modern
n nightclub
o overtime
p package
q quality
r renovations
s staff
t tariff
u underground
v voucher
w wildlife

Dealing with guests

Unit Notes

Exercise 1, page 40

Focus students' attention on the picture and ask them what they can see. Ask students *Would you like to be a hotel manager? Why (not)?* Check the students understand *charming* (positive meaning: pleasant; negative meaning: someone who uses their attractiveness to influence people), *a clown, routine detail* and *a sense of humour* (ability to see things as amusing). Students order the characteristics individually before discussing their ideas with a partner.

Exercise 2, page 40

Students discuss the question in pairs and make a short list of two or three more characteristics. They justify their ideas in a brief class discussion.

Exercise 3, page 40

Students read the article and underline the characteristics in exercise 1 that are mentioned. They confirm their answers with a partner.

- like people: can deal with different kinds of people, share other people's feelings and empathise with their situation
- likes variety
- thinks like a child: is energetic and enthusiastic
- is like a clown: can excite others to find work pleasurable and fulfilling
- understands body language

Exercise 4, page 40

Give students time to read the text more carefully before putting them in pairs to answer. Encourage students to guess the meaning of new words from the context.

1 d **2** c **3** b

Exercise 5, page 41

Tell students that all the words appear in the first four exercises as either a noun, adjective or verb. Check the students understand the meaning of the nouns by defining each one. Students complete the exercise in pairs, using their knowledge and referring to the previous exercises for help. They can use a dictionary to finish the exercise. Get students to mark the stress on the new words. Practise the new words by repetition drilling.

Ask if anyone can explain the difference between *-ed* and *-ing* adjectives (in a monolingual class this is probably best done through translation). Elicit other adjectives which can be both, e.g. *frightening* / *frightened, surprising* / *surprised, exciting* / *excited, boring* / *bored, interesting* / *interested.*

charm	charming	charm
excellence	excellent	excel
enthusiasm	enthusiastic	enthuse
fulfil(l)ment	fulfilling / fulfilled	fulfil(l)
pleasure	pleasurable / pleasant	please
success	successful	succeed
variety	various	vary

Workbook: Word-building, page 26, exercises 2 and 3.

Exercise 6, page 41

Fact File

A *housekeeper* in a hotel is responsible for the preparation of guest rooms and the cleanliness of all public areas of the hotel. Requests for extra blankets and other services are often passed on to housekeeping. They need to liaise closely with reception so that rooms are available for guests as quickly as possible.

Check students understand *a quality* (a positive characteristic). Students discuss the question in pairs or small groups. Encourage students to justify their ideas.

Extra Activity

• With a less confident group, review the language needed for this speaking activity by doing the first one as a class. Write any good expressions that students use on the board and rephrase any incorrectly formed sentences:

must / should	*be able to*
	have the ability to
	have good ... skills
	be + adjective
	pay attention to ...

• Alternative: Pyramid discussion. In pairs, students decide on the four most important skills / qualities for one of the jobs. They then join another pair and compare and justify their ideas. Give the groups a few minutes to agree. Continue joining the groups until the whole class has the same four characteristics for the job.

• If your students are working in the tourism industry now or have had any work experience in it, ask them to explain what skills and qualities these jobs need. It may also be interesting to ask what they think are the characteristics of a good teacher!

Language focus, page 42

Get students to underline all the examples of *a*, *the* and nouns without an article in front in the text on page 41 of the Students' Book. There is no need to check answers here. When students have added the examples to the rules, ask them to highlight the ones that are different from their language. Direct the students to the language summary on page 126 for further examples.

• *a* before professions: *a psychologist*
• *the* before a previously-mentioned noun: *in a recent study... the study showed*
• *the* before noun identified by a phrase or clause that follows: *the characteristics that make hoteliers not just good but excellent*
• no article when countable, plural nouns are used in general sense: *hoteliers* (This is also true for uncountable nouns used in a general sense, e.g. *Time is money*.)
• superlative expressions: *the most successful*

Workbook: Articles, page 27, exercises 5 and 6.

Exercise 7, page 42

Ask students to look at the pairs of words and count the number of syllables in each word. They can then identify and mark the stressed syllables. Encourage students to check their answers using a dictionary before going through them as a class.

Exercise 8, page 43

It is important with this exercise that students understand the full context before attempting to complete the gaps. Ask students to read the emails and summarise them with a partner first. Then, working together, they can go back and add articles where necessary. Encourage students to guess the meaning of new words from the context where possible: *a motel* (a hotel by the side of the road for people who are travelling by car), *to shout, to foresee* (predict), *a kid, floors* (in a hotel), *to invade* (enter in large numbers), *autograph hunters, the paparazzi* (the photographers who follow famous people everywhere they go), *to prevent* (stop), *a threat to someone's privacy* (something that seems likely to endanger that privacy), *in the public eye* (you are a famous person who is written about in newspapers and magazines and seen on TV), *to take steps* (take action). To avoid a lengthy feedback, put the answers on the board as students are finishing and only go over the ones where students had difficulties.

1 no article (generalisation) OR *the* noise *at motels* (identified by the phrase following it)
2 no article (plural noun, generalisation)
3 an (not specific)
4 no article (plural noun, generalisation)
5 no article (plural noun, generalisation)
6 no article (plural noun, generalisation)
7 a (one of more)
8 no article (plural noun, generalisation)
9 the (singular countable noun, generalisation, e.g. *the computer* has changed the way we work)
10 no article OR The

11 a (one of more)
12 no article (plural noun, generalisation)
13 the (fixed expression)
14 the (identified by phrase that follows: of any guest)
15 the (fixed expression)
16 a (with expressions of quantity, e.g. *a lot of, a few of*)
17 the (specific, is clear which one from context)
18 the (identified by phrase that follows: of paying on departure)
19 the (specific, is clear which one from context)
20 the (specific, is clear which one from context)
21 no article (plural noun, generalisation)

Exercise 9, page 43

Students discuss their ideas in pairs or small groups. They could then compare their ideas with another pair / group or as a class and decide on the best response to each question.

Exercise 10, page 43

This writing task should take about ten minutes in class or could be set for homework. Refer students to page 122 of the Writing bank in the Students' Book. Discuss how they could start and finish the email, e.g. *Geoff, this is a very common problem and I am not sure what the answer is.* At the end they should put their name and city. You may also wish to elicit / introduce some language for making suggestions, e.g. *Have you thought about -ing? I suggest you + verb* (without *to*). Students exchange their finished emails with a partner who checks for grammar and spelling mistakes.

> While these emails are fairly informal, the same type of website in other countries may be more formal in tone.

Extra Activity

Advice for hoteliers can be found at www.newhotelier.co.uk in 'Old Hands Wisdom'. Each month a different hotelier is asked to give their advice. Students could read and summarise the advice and say whether they agree or disagree. Alternatively, give students different parts of the feature which they then summarise and discuss with their partner.

Exercise 11, page 44

Put the title of the book on the board and ask students to guess what the book is about. Students read the introduction and discuss the questions as a class. You could use the questions for a quick scan reading of the text.

the financier's wife suffered from altitude sickness, a symptom of which is headaches; the hotel provided oxygen bottles in the rooms.

Exercise 12, page 44

Check words: *to improve, a lack of* (not have / not have enough of), *to release, to worsen, to lose your temper, to waste time.* Explain that students should try to work out the meaning of *red carpet treatment* and *the last straw* from the text. Set a time limit of two minutes for students to find the answers in the extract. Feed back as a class.

1 special treatment offered to very important guests
2 he had come to discuss important financial projects with the local government
3 'the last straw' is an extra problem that is added to a difficult or unpleasant situation and which makes you think you cannot tolerate the situation any longer. This was probably the last straw for the manager because it was a serious mistake involving an important guest.
4 she thought that the guest wanted to know if a Mr Oxygen was staying in the hotel and didn't realise that there was a problem with the extra oxygen supply in the room.
5 accept all reasonable ideas, e.g. basic hotel English courses provided for all staff.

Exercise 13, page 44

Give students five minutes to prepare their roles. Students A work together and students B work together. First, they should discuss the following questions: *What do you want from the meeting?* (For student A this might include a discount, compensation, some action taken to guarantee this type of problem will not arise again. For student B this might include pacification of the guest, restoring confidence in the hotel service, keeping the guest.) *How can you achieve this?* (Students should think about the tone and language of the conversation.) Students make notes on what they are going to say. Circulate and help where necessary. To make the meeting seem more authentic, seat the manager behind a table. Feed back briefly on the outcome of the meetings.

Exercise 14, page 45

Explain that all the expressions are about misunderstanding – when someone / something is understood wrongly. Students complete the exercise in pairs, using a dictionary, preferably a monolingual one, to help. Ask students if the expressions translate into their own language. Students use some of the expressions to make sentences true to the story on page 44 of the Students' Book, e.g. the operator and the guest were talking at cross purposes.

- *miss the point* – not understand what is the most important part
- *talk at cross purposes, get your / our / their lines crossed* – when two people are talking about different things but they think they are talking about the same thing
- *get the wrong end of the stick* – to misunderstand completely what has been said
- *not make head nor tail of something* – not be able to understand something at all

1 point **2** cross **3** stick **4** crossed **5** tail

Extra Activity
- Alternatively, if your students are unfamiliar with the expressions, you could present them first on the board with books closed and then use the exercise as practice. In this case, write the complete expressions on the board. Students use a dictionary, preferably a monolingual one, to discover the differences in meaning between the expressions, then continue as above.
- Students imagine they are the guest from the story on page 44. They write a letter of complaint to the manager of the hotel, including at least one of the expressions.

Workbook: Misunderstanding, page 28, exercise 8.

Exercise 15, page 45

Students predict the order before listening to check. Check words: *show someone to a room, to report* (officially tell), *a necklace, to unpack*. Remind students that they should number the events in the order that they *occur* and not the order they hear them on the cassette / CD. The listening is in five parts. After each section, pause the cassette for students to compare what they have heard with a partner.

1 the receptionist misunderstands the name
2 Mrs Horton goes to room 112
3 Mrs Horton unpacks her clothes and uses the bathroom
4 the porter shows Mrs Horton to room 212
5 Mrs Horton reports the missing necklace to reception
6 the receptionist offers to ring the housekeeper
7 Mrs Horton telephones her husband

Exercise 16, page 45

Explain that students are going to summarise orally the events so far. They listen again for any extra information and / or useful vocabulary / expressions. Students should be familiar with the sequencing and reason / result words. Give them a few minutes to make notes on what they are going to say. They close their books and use their notes.

Extra Activity
Students use sections 1, 2 and 4 of the tapescript on page 133 of the Students' Book and role-play the receptionist and Mrs Horton. Circulate and monitor pronunciation and intonation.

Exercise 17, page 45

Students predict the answers to the first five questions and then listen to check. Replay any parts of the dialogue if students have missed anything or got something wrong. Feed back as a class, including their ideas on what the receptionist should do next. Elicit that one of the things he / she should do is inform the Duty Manager of what has happened.

1 it was either lost or stolen
2 where his wife is
3 the necklace was mislaid while moving rooms and the housekeeper searched the first room but was unable to find the necklace
4 his wife has been moved to a different room
5 the switchboard didn't know that the room had been changed

Exercise 18, page 45

Fact File

The *Duty Manager* in a hotel is the most senior manager working in the front office (reception). Their main responsibility is dealing with guests, getting problems solved and dealing with complaints and queries.

Students work in pairs. Refer students to page 118 of the Writing bank in the Students' Book. Give the students five minutes to note what they want to include in the memo and organise their ideas. Students then compare their ideas with another pair and comment on any unnecessary information / omissions. Circulate and monitor. Point out that the formality of a memo depends on the relationship between the two people. In this situation, it probably needs to be semi-formal. Discuss how students could start (just with the Duty Manager's first name) and finish (*Regards, Best wishes, See you tomorrow*) the memo. Set a time limit of ten minutes for students to write the memo in class, or ask students to write the final version for homework.

Exercise 19, page 46

Ask students *Have you ever complained about the condition of your room when you were staying in a hotel? What was the problem? What types of room problems might a guest complain about?* Students compare their ideas with the list in the Students' Book. Be prepared to explain / translate: *disgusting, a sheet, stained, torn, dusty, stuck, faucet* (US English, UK English: *tap*), *to drip*. Encourage students to work out the meaning of new words in the responses from the context. As students listen to check, get them to repeat the response and focus on the pronunciation of '*ll*. To help them make this sound, encourage them to insert an extra /j/ sound so /aɪl/ becomes /aɪjl/.

> 1 a 2 h 3 c 4 f 5 e 6 g 7 d 8 b

> **Extra Activity**
> - Students work in pairs, A and B. Student A covers the complaints and only looks at the responses. Student B reads a complaint and A chooses / recalls the appropriate response. Alternatively, student A closes their book and attempts to respond appropriately, with B prompting where necessary.
> - With large classes put the complaints and responses on cards. Give each student a card and then get them to mingle in order to find their partner with the right card.
> - Elicit different room complaints using the same vocabulary, e.g. *the air-conditioning is making a funny noise. The shower tap is dripping. I asked for a hairdryer in the room.* Students practise responding to these complaints.

Workbook: Hotel problems, page 28, exercise 7.

Professional practice, page 46

Ask students how they would deal with a guest who had a complaint: *Where would they talk to the guest? What would they say? How would they say it?* Students compare their ideas with the ones in the Students' Book. Check students understand: *to raise your voice* (speak angrily). Encourage students to attempt to match the phrases with the advice before checking the exact meaning of some phrases: *to look into the matter* (investigate), *to see to something* (deal with), *straightaway*.

> 1 Thank you for bringing the matter to my attention.
> 2 I'm (very / terribly) sorry.
> 3 I do apologise for the inconvenience.
> 4 What seems to have happened is that ...
> 5 There's been a misunderstanding.
> 6 There seems to have been a problem / a mix-up.
> 7 We'll look into the matter and ...
> 8 I suggest that we ...
> 9 I'll see to it straightaway.

Exercise 20, page 47

Pre-teach: *bring the wrong order, the remote control, to leak, an insect.* Give students five minutes preparation time. Student A reads and remembers the complaints on page 47 of the Students' Book. Student B reviews the language of dealing with complaints on page 46. To give the role-play a more authentic feel, have the receptionist standing behind a 'reception desk'. The guest can decide whether to make the complaint face-to-face or over the phone. As they do this, circulate and note down errors / useful language. Feed back on these before the students reverse roles so that they can incorporate the suggestions and corrections.

Exercise 21, page 47

Students discuss the question in pairs. If they write a list, ask the pair with the longest list to feed back.

> **Suggested answers**
> an extra night free, a discount on the price, a discount on a future reservation, complimentary drinks / excursion / tickets for a show

Exercise 22, page 47

This activity should take about 20 minutes. Divide the students into *As* and *Bs*.

A students work together in small groups. Refer them to page 115 of the Students' Book. Give them a few minutes to read the introduction, before checking comprehension: *Do you have confirmation of your reservation? When did you book the rooms for? What do you need to do now?* Allow a further five minutes to prepare the party information and consider how they are going to express their complaint.

B students work together in small groups. Give them a few minutes to read the introduction and study the reservations chart. Check words: *in charge of, room allocation / to allocate, proof* (something to show that what they say is true). Check comprehension by asking: *What are you going to ask for first? What are you going to do for the guests? Why don't you want to give them any superior rooms?* Point out that they need to think of an explanation for how the mistake happened. Allow a further five minutes for them to prepare this and think about the language involved.

Pair up *A* and *B* students. For a more authentic feel, seat the reservations clerk behind a 'desk'. Students role-play the conversation from welcoming the guest into the office to finding a solution and concluding. Circulate and make a note of errors / useful language for analysis later. Feed back briefly on the solutions agreed to in each of the pairs.

Extra Activity

Following the language feedback from the role-play, students repeat the activity with a different partner. Encourage them to incorporate any suggestions and / or corrections and set a five minute time limit to make the role-play more challenging.

P. **Photocopiable extra, see page 84**

Dealing with a complaint

You will need one copy of the hotel guest role card and one copy of the hotel manager role card for each pair of students.

Language: dealing with complaints

- Put students into pairs and give one student a copy of the hotel guest role card and the other a copy of the hotel manager role card. Allow students a couple of minutes to read the information and check the useful expressions.

- Organise the tables and chairs so that each pair can sit either side of a desk, resembling the hotel manager's office. Students do the role-play in pairs.

- Students report to the class on the compensation offered by each hotel manager.

6 Travel agencies

UNIT OBJECTIVES

Professional practice:	Take a telephone booking
	Prepare an educational report
	Reply to an enquiry
Language focus:	The future
Vocabulary:	Telephone language
	The word *time*

Unit Notes

Fact File

Travel agencies are shops which sell holidays and travel products, such as car hire, airline tickets, theatre tickets, etc.

Exercise 1, page 48

Students look at the picture and describe what they can see. Highlight that the place is called a *travel agency* and the person who works there a *travel agent* or *travel sales consultant*. Ask students what type of conversations travel agents have on the phone, e.g. confirming prices with an airline. Elicit / Teach the differences between *deal with / make enquiries* and *take / make bookings*. Students discuss the question in pairs or small groups. If necessary, prompt them to discuss the information they need to give, the information they need to ask for, the details they need to check, their manner. You may wish to refer to telephone language on page 49 of the Students' Book during feedback.

Exercise 2, page 48

Students read the booking form and check what information they are listening for. Point out that next to 'party members' they just need to write a number. Warn the students that they may not hear the information in the same order as it is on the booking form. Reading the booking form through once more will help students remember the information they are listening for. Play the recording once straight through. Students compare their answers in pairs. Play the cassette again, pausing as necessary.

1	BT 5473
2	8.05
3	Barajas
4	16/4
5	17.50
6	single
7	3
8	*1*
9	G
10	Jones
11	SE4 7PG
12	07702 623479

Extra Activity

For less confident students you may wish to review how dates are written and spoken in English before doing the listening. The date can be written *17(th) March 2004* or *March 17(th) 2004* or *17/03/04* or *03/17/04* (in the US the date is written month / day / year). However, in speaking it is *the seventeenth of March, two thousand and four* or *March the seventeenth, two thousand and four*. Elicit some more dates from students and demonstrate the written and spoken form. Point out the difference between the voiced sound /ð/ in *the* and the unvoiced sound /θ/ in *third, fifteenth, twenty-fifth, thirty-first*.

Exercise 3, page 48

Drill the pronunciation of the seven sounds and the example letters. Students could predict the pronunciation of the other letters before listening to the cassette to confirm. Check accurate pronunciation during class feedback. Point out that z is pronounced /zed/ in UK English and /ziː/ in US English.

/eɪ/	A H J K
/iː/	B C D E G P T V
/e/	F L M N S X Z
/aɪ/	I Y
/əʊ/	O
/uː/	Q U W
/ɑː/	R

<table>
<tr><td>

Extra Activity
- Students dictate short sentences to each other, letter by letter. Their partner reports their sentence back to them. Dictate a sentence of your own to the class first as an example.
- Students role-play the conversation from exercise 2. More confident students can use the booking form as a prompt. Less confident students can use the tapescript on page 134 of the Students' Book.

</td></tr>
</table>

Exercise 4, page 49

Draw students' attention to the vocabulary diagram. Ask students to tick the expressions they already know and underline any new expressions. Students work individually or in pairs before checking answers with the whole class.

> **1** dead on time **2** in time **3** in good time
> **4** estimated time of arrival **5** right time **6** at any one time **7** time zones **8** take your time

<table>
<tr><td>

Extra Activity
Students write true sentences using some of the expressions, e.g. *I arrived in good time for this English class.* They could then read them to a partner, leaving a gap where the 'time' phrase is. The listener says the expression which is missing. Demonstrate with an example of your own first.

</td></tr>
</table>

Workbook: Time, page 31, exercise 3.

Professional practice, page 49

Students read the 'telephone language' tips and say if they agree with the advice. Check comprehension of the useful phrases by asking students to express in other words: *put you through* (connect you), *the line's engaged / busy* (the person is talking on the phone to someone else), *hold* (wait). Drill the pronunciation of the sentences.

Workbook: Telephone language, page 68, exercise 12.

Exercise 5, page 49

This exercise gives students the opportunity to put into practice the telephone tips and language and it gives you the opportunity to assess the students' competence with future forms. Allow ten minutes for students to prepare their role.

Students *A* read the information on page 110. Also, refer them to the 'telephone language' tips. Students *B* prepare questions in pairs or small groups. Monitor and help as necessary. During the conversation, make a note of language used well / errors for analysis and / or correction

later. Feed back briefly on whether student *B* thinks the weekend break is attractive or not and why.

Tips: To role-play telephone conversations, have students sitting back-to-back. That way, as in a real telephone conversation, they cannot use any visual clues. It also means that students have to speak louder so it is easier to monitor.

<table>
<tr><td>

Extra Activity
More confident pairs can continue the conversation, with student *A* taking the booking for student *B*.

</td></tr>
</table>

Language focus, page 50

If necessary translate the uses of the verb forms before getting the students to do the matching activity in pairs or groups. During feedback, confirm which verb form is necessary for each use. Read aloud the summary of the verb forms and their uses. Illustrate them further with personal examples and elicit some examples from students. Point out that when the main verb with *going to* is *go*, it is commonly omitted, e.g. *We're going to go to Greece this summer. This is often pronounced as* /gɒnə gəʊ/.

Draw attention to the uses of the future continuous. Point out that the future continuous is usually interchangeable with the present continuous for arrangements that have already been made, e.g. *We'll be leaving / We are leaving for Tokyo tomorrow morning, Jan will be giving / is giving the first presentation at the conference.*

<table>
<tr><td>

Language note
- Students may find the 'prediction' label unsatisfactory for some sentences, e.g. *He'll have more responsibility in his new job.* 'Prediction' is used broadly here to mean something you see as inevitable / a future fact.
- Students may find the difference between the present continuous and *going to* difficult to see. This is partly because the uses of the two forms do overlap: *going to* can almost always be used instead of the present continuous. However, the present continuous cannot be used where there is just a vague intention, there must be some kind of arrangement. For example: *I'm going to phone the car hire company tomorrow, I'm going to visit my family in Australia when I finish my degree* or *Before I go to Egypt, I'm going to learn some Arabic* cannot be put in the present continuous.

</td></tr>
</table>

> **1** d **2** b **3** a **4** e **5** c

Extra Activity

The forms should be familiar but it may be useful to remind students of the following points:

- contraction of *will* ('*ll*) and *will not* (*won't*)
- the difference in form between the present continuous and *going to* (with *going to* the main verb is in the infinitive)
- the future continuous is formed with *will / won't + be + -ing*

Workbook: The future, pages 31 and 32, exercises 4 and 5.

Exercise 6, page 50

Students work individually or in pairs to complete the dialogue. Encourage students to resolve any differences of opinion with their partner by justifying their choices.

> **1** leaves **2** will I be staying **3** 'll be staying
> **4** going to ring **5** will be paying **6** 'll put **7** 'll get

---

Extra Activity

Students role-play the conversation. With a more confident group, note the key words of the conversation on the board. Students then cover the dialogue and practise it in pairs, using only the key words to help them. Make sure they swap roles. Tell them they don't need to remember the exact words of the dialogue.

P. **Photocopiable extra, page 85**

Futures game

You will need one copy of the sentences for each pair of students.

Language: future tenses

- Before starting, tell students about Air Miles. In the UK some companies and services are affiliated with Air Miles. As a result, customers can earn air miles when they buy that company's products or use their services, e.g. when they shop in a supermarket, stay in a hotel, use a credit card, etc. The air miles are 'saved' in an account and can later be used to pay for flights. Ask students if there is anything similar in their country.

- Put students in pairs or small groups. Give each pair / group the list of twelve sentences. Explain that some of the sentences are grammatically correct and some are incorrect. The aim of the game is to identify whether the sentence is correct or not and so win air miles. The winners are the group with the most air miles. They will be able to choose a destination within the range of their air miles.

- They start with 50 air miles. They bet air miles on whether the sentence is correct or incorrect. The bets should be multiples of ten. The maximum bet at any time is 100 air miles. If they guess correctly they double their bet. If they guess incorrectly they lose their bet. If they can correct an incorrect sentence, they get a bonus 50 air miles.

> **1** incorrect. I'll look it up.
> **2** correct
> **3** incorrect. How are you getting / will you be getting there?
> **4** incorrect. How will you be paying?
> **5** incorrect. The show starts
> **6** correct
> **7** incorrect. I'll make a note
> **8** correct
> **9** incorrect. I'm going to write it up.
> **10** correct
> **11** incorrect. We will deliver
> **12** incorrect. are starting / are going to start

Exercise 7, page 51

Ask students if they know what an educational report is. If they don't, set a time limit of one minute for them to find out and answer the question.

> *They are for members of staff of travel agencies.*

Exercise 8, page 51

Check the meaning of *aim* (objective, reason for). Students work individually or in pairs before checking their answers with the class. Encourage students to guess new vocabulary from context: *share, stage, feedback session*.

> **1** to help staff recommend destinations to their customers
> **2** complete a questionnaire using the Tour Operator's brochure
> **3** complete the Educational Booklet
> **4** information about the resort, the travel arrangements and the hotel
> **5** discuss the trip with your manager and how you are going to train the other members of staff during the feedback session

Exercise 9, page 51

Tell students they are going to prepare an educational report. The preparation stage will take 45 minutes. It is best done in class where students can discuss their ideas and how to express them. However, if you are short of time or have short classes, you could set the research part for homework. Each presentation itself should be about five minutes, though this depends on the size and level of the class.

Write the three topics which should be covered in an educational report on the board: *the resort*, *travel arrangements* and *the hotel*. For each of these topics, elicit a question which should be answered in the report and write it under the topic, e.g.

THE RESORT
What are the main attractions?

Organise the students into pairs or small groups and assign them one of the topics. Give the pairs / groups 5–10 minutes to write more questions on that topic. Feed back and write all the questions on the board. Students compare these to the questions on page 51 of the Students' Book. Check students understand the meaning of *selling points*.

Students copy the questions from the board. They should aim to answer these questions in their report. To research a destination the following websites are useful: www.lonelyplanet.com, www.roughguides.com and www.timeout.com. Alternatively, students can use a search engine, such as yahoo.com or excite.com. At all of these websites, students can also find some information about hotels. Students could work individually, though it is probably best in pairs or in groups to allow more collaboration and discussion. If your students don't have access to the internet, bring in information on different destinations or students could do a report on a place they are familiar with.

Once the students have made their notes for the report, give them ten minutes to organise them and practise presenting them with their partner / group. Monitor and help as necessary.

For the presentation of the reports, organise students in groups of 6–8, with the speaker in the middle of a horseshoe, similar to the set-up for a meeting. Encourage listeners to ask questions at the end of each report. When all the reports have been heard, feed back on which one was the most interesting, the best presented, the best researched, which place they would most like to visit, etc.

Extra Activity

Ask listening students to refer to the list of questions from the beginning of the class and check that they are all answered by the speaker.

Exercise 10, page 52

Fact File

A *corrida* is Spanish for a bullfight.

Tell students they are going to look at a city guide for Madrid. Ask *Has anyone been to Madrid? What do you know about / associate with Madrid?* Ask students *What information do you expect to find in a city guide?* They quickly compare their ideas to the headings. Don't explain the headings at this stage. Set a time limit of one minute for students to match the headings and paragraphs. During feedback, ask students to identify which words in the text led them to the answer.

1 F 2 G 3 D 4 B 5 E 6 C 7 A 8 H

Exercise 11, page 53

Students answer the questions in pairs. Emphasise that they do not need to understand all the vocabulary to answer the questions.

1 You don't have enough time to see it all.
2 Because there are so many people it's almost impossible to move.
3 False. It's a place to go to listen to flamenco guitar and cante singing.
4 By taxi, bus or metro.
5 They don't serve meals.
6 Because it is a very old city with narrow streets and lots to see.

Exercise 12, page 53

Students quickly scan the text to find the answers.

- 6th century – the Visigoths made Toledo their capital.
- The Middle Ages – Toledo was a melting pot of Christian, Muslim and Jewish cultures.
- 12th–19th century – The Prado Museum has Spanish paintings from this period.
- 19th century – El Rastro was popular.
- 11 am – Madrilenos have their second breakfast, often in a bar or a café.
- 3 pm – Madrilenos have their lunch.
- every 12 minutes – the airport bus goes to Plaza de Colón

Extra Activity

- Alternatively, get students to close their books. Divide them into teams. Write the dates and times on the board. In their teams, students try to recall the significance of each. Award one point for a well-formed sentence and one point if the information is correct.
- Write the following questions on the board for the students to discuss:

How would you spend a weekend in Madrid?
What is the most attractive part of the description of the city?

Travel guide project

Students write a text about their own city / area based on the Madrid model. Discuss eight possible headings and the contents of each as a class, supplying useful vocabulary. The writing could be set as homework.

Exercise 13, page 54

Focus students' attention on the pictures and get them to speculate about what the members of the Evans family would like to do in Madrid. Students read the profile to find out if they were correct. Check the meaning of *to collect*, *to tolerate* (to allow or accept something that you do not like or agree with), *occasional*, *sightseeing*. Check students understand the word *an itinerary* (plan of a journey, route or visit). Students prepare the itinerary in pairs or small groups.

Extra Activity

- With a less confident group you may want to remind them of expressions for making suggestions, e.g. *They could ...*, *They should ...*, agreeing and disagreeing: *Yes, that's a good idea, I agree, I'm not sure about that*, etc.
- With more confident students, you could give them an information update in the middle of the activity, e.g. *the weather forecast is for snow, the Prado shuts at 3 pm on Sunday, there are some tickets left to see Spain's top bullfighter in action on Saturday afternoon.*
- Students regroup, listen to each other's itineraries and decide which is the best.
- Students role-play a conversation between the tour operator and Mr / Mrs Evans. Mr / Mrs Evans starts, *'Hello. This is Mr / Mrs Evans. I'm phoning to check the itinerary for our weekend in Madrid'.*

Exercise 14, page 55

Fact File

- *Service charges* refers to the cost which is added for the service you receive in a hotel.
- *Porterage* refers to the cost of transferring luggage.

Check the meaning of *request*. Explain that this letter is a response to a request. Ask students to read the letter quickly and work out what the customer's original request was (for information on escorted journeys to Central and Eastern Europe). Check words: *escorted, requirements, to require, highlights*. Students complete the letter in pairs. Remind students of the conventions of a formal letter in English (see Students' Book page 120).

1. Thank you for your recent request
2. I am pleased to enclose
3. included in the price
4. £100 off the brochure price
5. There is current availability
6. make the necessary arrangements
7. please do not hesitate to contact us
8. Yours sincerely

Extra Activity

Ask further comprehension questions on the letter, e.g. *What does the travel consultant send with the letter? How could Mr and Mrs Blake get a discount?*

Exercise 15, page 55

This activity should take about 50–60 minutes. The writing of the final copy could be set for homework, however the planning is best done in class so that the students can discuss and improve their drafts.

Elicit what type of holidays a tour operator might specialise in, e.g. luxury holidays, cultural holidays, family holidays, activity holidays, budget travelling, etc. Organise students into pairs and ask them to decide what type of holiday their company specialises in. Give them ten minutes to make notes on the information they are going to include in the letter about weekend breaks in their city.

Allow students a further ten minutes to organise their notes and think about the language they are going to use, referring to the useful phrases on page 55 of the Students' Book.

Students then explain these ideas to another pair. Write the following questions on the board for the listeners to answer:

Is the information well-organised?
Is there too little / not enough information?
Are they going to send a brochure?

Based on the feedback, students then write the first draft. This should take 15–20 minutes. They should then exchange their first draft with a different pair. This time the readers check the draft against the writing tips on page 55 of the Students' Book, i.e. *Is the letter friendly and positive?* etc. Circulate and monitor these evaluations. It may be useful to highlight good examples of language and / or general weaknesses to the class.

Tips: If your students are reluctant to appraise each other's work, make the feedback question less open-ended, e.g. *Find two ways in which you think the letter could be improved.*

When students have written their final copy, follow up by asking students to compare their letters and decide who seems to offer the most attractive deal. Students could also compare their letters with the following suggested answer:

> **Suggested answer**
> Dear Ms Mellor
>
> Thank you for your recent request for information about weekend breaks in Madrid. I am pleased to enclose a brochure with detailed information on the attractions of Madrid, travel arrangements and accommodation.
> We specialise in culinary weekend breaks in Spain. The weekend in Madrid is one of our most popular holidays. Accommodation is in a five-star, stylish hotel situated on the main avenue. Friday evening is spent wine-tasting with an experienced *sumiller*. Among the delights planned for the weekend, participants try out the famed seafood from Galicia and eat in a Michelin-star Basque restaurant. They also have the opportunity to admire the attractions of Madrid while enjoying the varied *tapas*. The group is always accompanied by one of our experts and is never more than eight people.
> We are currently offering a 20% discount off the brochure price for holidays that are booked and paid for before the end of the month.
> If you require any further information, please do not hesitate to contact us. I look forward to hearing from you.
>
> Yours sincerely
> Joanna Bright

Extra Activity
- Alternatively, bring in some brochures for weekend breaks abroad and students write their letters based on information in these.
- Students role-play a meeting between the representative of an overseas tour operator and the manager of the local tour operator. The overseas tour operator is interested in sending customers on weekend breaks in the city and would like more information about options offered by the local tour operator. Give the students five minutes to prepare their roles.

Hotel reservations

UNIT OBJECTIVES

Professional practice:	Take messages
	Send text messages
	Sell a conference venue
	Write a formal letter
Language focus:	Reported speech, indirect questions
Vocabulary:	Text messaging, Conferences and conventions

Unit Notes

Exercise 1, page 56

Focus students' attention on the picture and ask them what they can see. Discuss the question as a class and write the students' ideas on the board.

> The basic information is When? How long? Who? What type of room? In addition they may also ask for a phone / fax number, an address and postcode, the company the guest is with, payment details, flight details, arrival time, car registration number, nationality, smoker / non-smoker, whether the guest has stayed in the hotel before.

Exercise 2, page 56

In pairs, students decide on a possible order. Before listening to check the order, explain that they will not hear all the questions and some of the questions may be phrased differently on the cassette / CD.

> In questions b and c, *would* can be replaced by *will*. *Would* makes the question sound more formal.

1 f **2** c **3** g **4** e **5** a

Extra Activity

With a more confident group, get students to write their own list of questions that they think will be asked, reviewing both question forms and the use of the future continuous to ask questions politely. They then listen and order the ones they hear and add any extras. Highlight when one version of the question is more polite or formal than another.

Exercise 3, page 56

Students read the reservations screen and complete any answers they already know. Check the students understand the abbreviations SGL (single), DBL (double), TWB (twin-bedded) and that the # symbol means *number*. Check words: *suite* /swiːt/ (a set of rooms in a hotel; bedroom, bathroom and sitting-room), *rate* (cost per person / room per night). Tell students that they will not hear the information in the order on the reservations screen. Reading the reservations form through once more will help students remember the information they are listening for. Play the cassette / CD, pausing at regular intervals to allow students to compare their answers with a partner. Replay any parts which they are unsure about. Feed back as a class.

1	15th July
2	2
3	Herridge
4	Ann
5	2
6	none
7	25 Oldham Road, Manchester
8	DBL
9	non-smoking
10	205
11	£110 per person
12	bottle of champagne in room on arrival
13	yes
14	103
15	VISA
16	4999 1825 6857 6238

Extra Activity

Students role-play the telephone conversation between Ann Herridge and the reservations agent. Less confident students could use the tapescript. More confident students could use the reservations screen as a prompt.

Exercise 4, page 57

This is similar to exercise 3 except the conversation takes place at the reception desk rather than over the phone and the registration card is not computerised. Again, warn the students that they will not hear the information in the same order as on the registration card. Play the cassette / CD straight through the first time. Students compare their answers. Repeat the listening, pausing where necessary to confirm answers.

1 6/12
2 8/12
3 19
4 £95 per night incl. breakfast
5 double room with a bath
6 Urbanik
7 Polish
8 EG6662781
9 Credit card

Workbook: Checking in / out, page 66, exercise 7.

Exercise 5, page 57

Point out that how you say something is often just as important as the words you choose. Students listen and decide whether the speaker sounds polite or impolite. Feed back as a class. As students are practising, circulate and monitor.

1 P 2 I 3 P 4 P 5 I 6 P 7 I 8 I

Exercise 6, page 57

Students predict the stressed words before listening to check. Elicit / Point out that the stressed words are the ones that give the main message of the sentence, in this case the two alternatives. Students practise saying the sentences.

1 Will that be one or two nights?
2 We're arriving on the 15th and leaving on the 17th.
3 Would you like a single or a double room?
4 Would you prefer smoking or non-smoking rooms?
5 Is the room at the back or the front of the hotel?

Workbook: Contrastive stress, page 36, exercise 4.

Language focus: page 58

Continuing on the theme of politeness, point out that an indirect question is more polite than a direct question. Students look at the examples. Elicit that the word order in the second part of an indirect question is like a normal statement. Point out that if the direct question is a Yes / No question then the second part starts with the word *if* or *whether*. Highlight also that there is no need for a question mark at the end of an indirect question starting *I was wondering*. Point out the use of the past tense to make a question more polite / respectful.

Extra Activity

With less confident students, write the following structure on the board for students to refer to:

Do you know	*if / whether*	Subject + verb …?
Do you have any idea	*when*	
Could you tell me	*how much*	
I was wondering	*what time*	

Workbook: Indirect questions, page 36, exercise 5.

Exercise 7, page 58

Check words: *a connecting room, a florist's, a case, to vacate*. Students do the exercise individually or in pairs. When feeding back, monitor the intonation: it should fall at the end of indirect questions.

1 what the room rates are, please
2 if it is possible to have a connecting room
3 there is a florist's near here
4 if I can leave my cases here after I've vacated the room
5 how long the taxi will take to arrive

Exercise 8, page 58

Check words: *to settle a bill* (pay). Students do the exercise individually or in pairs.

1 Could you tell me / Do you know / Do you have any idea how much it costs to take a taxi to the airport?
2 I was wondering if I could settle the bill this evening.
3 Could you tell me / Do you know if there is a good bookshop near the hotel?

Exercise 9, page 58

Allow at least 20 minutes for this activity. Students *A* work together and students *B* work together. Pre-teach *a cot*. Give students five minutes to read their roles and check any vocabulary with their partner / group.

Check *B* students understand that a *TRB room* is a triple-bedded room. Give students a further five minutes to prepare the questions they are going to ask. Remind *B* students of the list of information needed by the reservations department, discussed in exercise 1. If you have access to the internet, you could print off a blank hotel booking form. Use a search engine, such as yahoo.com or excite.com. and search for 'hotel bookings'. Choose any hotel and there should be a blank reservation form to complete.

Remind all students to use indirect questions. During the role-play, circulate and monitor polite intonation. Note down errors / useful language for analysis and correction later. Feed back briefly on the solutions offered by the reservations clerks.

Tips: To role-play telephone conversations, have students sitting back-to-back. That way, as in a real telephone conversation, they cannot use any visual clues. It also means that students have to speak louder so it is easier to monitor.

Exercise 10, page 59

Ask students *Do you take / receive phone messages? In what situations? What is important when taking messages?* Compare their ideas with the ones in the Professional practice box. Students read Rosa's messages quickly. Can they understand the message? Play the cassette, pausing after each conversation for students to comment on the message.

- Message 1:
  name of the caller wrongly noted; Mr Young should specify which contract; for the Ashcroft deal the fax number is wrongly noted and not clear that it is a fax number; 1775 583 0182
- Message 2:
  Fine except it doesn't state 'tomorrow'
- Message 3
  Message to call him is not clear.
  Phone number is incorrect: 0660616350
  Message represented by drawing is not clear.

Extra Activity

- Students listen again and correct / rewrite Rosa's messages so they are more effective.
- With a strong class, get students to copy the outline of the message (From, To, Message, etc.) into their notebooks. Students listen to each conversation and complete the message form. They then compare their messages with the ones in the book and decide what are the positive and negative aspects of both.

Exercise 11, page 59

Play the conversations one at a time, pausing for students to discuss the question in pairs. Feed back as a class.

- Satisfactory message given to Mr Taylor.
- Can't give contract details to Mr Courtney and gives him the fax number instead of the phone number to call.
- Gives Ms Black the wrong mobile phone number for Brent Ross.

Language focus, page 60

In pairs, students predict the words that go in the spaces before listening again. Pause the cassette / CD after each of the sentences to give students time to check / correct / write their answer.

1 She said she would pick you up tomorrow at 8 o'clock.
2 He asked you to fax him a copy of the contract.
3 He said that his plane had been delayed.
4 He suggested that you phone him on his mobile.
5 He promised to get in touch again if there was a problem.
6 He told me to tell you that he loves / loved you very much.

In pairs, students decide if the rules are true or false, referring to the examples from the listening activity. Monitor their discussions and assess how much further clarification is necessary.

a false. In reported speech we do not usually repeat everything the person said, we just summarise it.
b true, e.g. suggest, promise.
c false . You can *say (that) something* or *tell someone (that) something,* e.g. He said (that) he was unhappy. He told me (that) he was unhappy. *Tell somebody to do something* is used to report an imperative. *Tell* must be followed by an object pronoun.
d true. The verb forms usually move one tense into the past.
e false. It is not always necessary to change the verb, e.g. for 6 you could write *He told me to tell you that he loves you very much.* It is possible to change the verb but it sounds formal. (Similarly time words only change if the time reference has changed between the direct speech and reporting it. Hence *tomorrow* in no.1 does not change.)

direct speech	indirect speech
present simple	⟶ past simple
present continuous	⟶ past continuous
present perfect	⟶ past perfect
past simple	⟶ past perfect
is going to	⟶ was going to
will	⟶ would
can	⟶ could
today	⟶ that day
tomorrow	⟶ the next day
yesterday	⟶ the day before

Workbook: Reported speech, page 36, exercise 6.

Exercise 12, page 60

Fact File

On a package holiday the client has a contract with the tour operator, not the hotel. It is therefore, in this situation, the tour operator's responsibility to compensate the client. The extent of the compensation would depend on Mrs Wood having proof of requesting a twin-bedded room when she booked the holiday and a receipt for the extra cost of the room. The consumer advice service may well recommend a legal adviser, specialised in the field of travel and holidays.

Before the students complete the spaces, get them to read through the text and summarise Mrs Wood's story to a partner. Encourage students to work out new words from the context: *to sort something out* (to find an answer to a problem), someone's *fault* (responsibility for a mistake), *a gesture of goodwill* (something you do to show friendly, helpful feelings towards another). Students then complete the exercise. Feed back as a class on the answers and the advice they would give Mrs Wood.

1 asked 2 told 3 could 4 said 5 was 6 told
7 added 8 would 9 promised

Exercise 13, page 61

Pre-teach *supposed to be doing something* (expected to do), *come to a standstill* (stop moving). Students read and check they understand the messages they have to pass on. Student *B* starts as the receptionist. Make sure the guest writes down the message so that they can check their comprehension at the end. Circulate and note down errors / useful language for analysis and correction later. Concentrate on the students' use of reported speech, though be aware that a tense change is not necessary in most of the cases. At the end, students compare their written notes to the original message.

Exercise 14, page 61

Discuss the following questions as a class: *Does everyone in the class have a mobile phone? Do they send text messages? When do they send text messages instead of phoning? What abbreviations do they use when they send text messages?* Write the example on the board and ask students if they can work out the message. Refer the students to the mini-glossary and get students to complete the exercise individually or in pairs. Use the example on the board to demonstrate reporting the message. Students check their answers by reporting them to another pair / their partner.

1 I'm late for a meeting. I'll see you at 10.
2 I'll see you at Kings Cross Station at 8. I hope you are OK.
3 Please send the pictures of the hotel room to John before tomorrow.
4 Can you tell me the time of the next meeting as soon as possible?
5 If you can't come, let me know as soon as possible. Thank you very much.
6 Your report is excellent. See you later.

Workbook: Text messages, page 37, exercise 8.

Exercise 15, page 61

Refer students to the glossary of text message abbreviations in the Students' Book on page 115. Give students 2–3 minutes to write their message and pass it on and then ask them to reply. If students have mobile phones they could use them to send and reply to the messages.

Extra Activity

After each student has sent a message and received a reply, they report the text message conversation to another student.

Exercise 16, page 62

Fact File

- A *conference* is a formal meeting or series of meetings between people who share the same interests. It often involves both lectures and discussion in smaller groups.
- A *convention* is a conference of people who do a particular job or who belong to a particular political party. The word is used especially in America.

Tell students that they are now going to look at organising conferences and conventions in hotels. Check the meaning of *catering*. In pairs or small groups, students categorise the words. Encourage students to teach each other new vocabulary instead of / before providing the answer yourself. The pronunciation of the following words may need particular attention: banquet /bæŋkwət/ , beverages /bevərɪdʒ/ , buffet /bʊfeɪ/ . Write the phonetics for words that students find difficult to pronounce on the board, marking the stress, and practise them by repetition drilling. Feed back on the answers and the students' additional ideas.

- places: auditorium, display area, meeting rooms
  possible extras: ballroom, conference room, exhibition hall
- equipment: flip chart, OHP *possible extras: video conferencing, slide projector, lectern* (sloping surface for holding a book or papers when reading in public), *public address* (PA) *system, autocue* (machine that allows a speaker to read words while looking at the audience)
- catering: à la carte, banquet, beverages, buffet, luncheon, refreshments
  possible extras: cocktail dinner, table d'hote meal (complete meal at a fixed price), *aperitif*

Extra Activity

Students research conference venues on the internet for more related vocabulary. The best way is to use a search engine, such as yahoo.com or excite.com and search for 'hotels for conferences'.

Workbook: Conferences, page 38, exercise 9 and page 70, exercise 16.

Exercise 17, page 62

This activity takes about 45 minutes. The preparation stage is best done in class where students can assist each other with comprehension and pool ideas. However, if you are short of time or have short classes, set the preparation for homework.

Start by asking students *What facilities does a hotel need if it wants to attract conferences? What other aspects of a hotel might a conference organiser be interested in?* (e.g. accessibility of hotel, sightseeing opportunities, etc.)

Students read the letter on page 62 of the Students' Book and underline the requirements for the conference. Be prepared to explain / translate: *a delegate* (a participant at a conference, a person chosen by a group to speak / vote for them), *an exhibitor, a plenary session* (a meeting when all the delegates are present), *a seminar* (an occasion when a teacher or expert and a group of people meet to study and discuss something), *a workshop* (small meeting to discuss and / or perform practical work in a subject), *a venue* (place where a public event or meeting happens).

Divide students into *A, B* and *C.* (If you have extra students, have more conference organisers. Try to choose more confident, imaginative students for *C,* which is the most challenging role.). Explain the roles to the students. Tell students that, while they will be allowed to refer to the Students' Book during the meeting, it will create a bad impression if they spend a lot of time looking for information. They should instead make notes and be familiar with the key information. Allow 10–15 minutes for this preparation stage.

A students work together in small groups, preparing questions for the two hotels. They should consider the possibility that both hotels can meet the requirements, in which case, what further factors could they ask about. Remind students that indirect questions are more polite.

B students work together in small groups. They read the information about the Magyar Hotel on page 63 of the Students' Book. Students discuss and make notes on how they can meet the requirements for the conference. In addition, what further selling points does the hotel have? Check words: *disabled facilities, laundry and valet service* (cleaning clothes).

C students work together in small groups. They read the information about the Plaza Casablanca hotel on page 112 of the Students' Book. Students discuss and make notes on how they can meet the requirements for the conference and what further selling points the hotel can offer. Check words: *lobby, theatre-style, cocktail dinner, mezzanine floor* (small additional floor between ground and first floor), *power socket, hanging closet* (small room for hanging clothes), *laundry and valet service*.

Put students in threes for the meeting. For a more authentic feel, have the conference organiser sitting at the head of a table with the two representatives either side. Students role-play the entire meeting from welcoming the two representatives to deciding which hotel is most suitable. The meeting should take 10–15 minutes. Circulate and note down errors / useful language for analysis and correction later. *A*s report briefly on which hotel they chose and why.

> **Extra Activity**
> If this area is of particular interest to your students, record one of the meetings on cassette or video. Replay the cassette / video, pausing to highlight / get students to identify good and weak points in the content and language of the discussion.

Exercise 18, page 63

This activity should take about 30 minutes. The writing of the final version could be set for homework, however the planning is best done in class so that the students can discuss and improve their drafts.

Keep students in the same groups of three as they were for the meeting (*A*, *B* and *C*) so that they don't have to repeat the decision-making and justification. Give students five minutes to make notes on the information they are going to include in the letter to TOEIT. Allow a further five minutes to organise their notes and think about the language they are going to use, reminding them of the conventions of formal letter writing. Refer students to pages 120 and 123 of the writing bank in the Students' Book. Students then write the first draft. This should only take ten minutes. They then exchange this first draft with a different group. Put the following questions on the board for the readers to answer:

Is the language and organisation suitable for a formal letter?
Is the information clear?
Is there enough information?
Is there any unnecessary information?

Circulate and monitor these evaluations. It may be useful to highlight good examples of language and / or general weaknesses to the class. Students then write a final copy of the letter.

(8) Seeing the sights

Unit Notes

Exercise 1, page 64

Focus students' attention on the pictures. In pairs, students match the pictures and types of tourist attractions. Ask them where they think each picture is and what they know about it.

> 1 festival 2 historic building 3 amusement park
> 4 safari park 5 place of natural beauty

Exercise 2, page 64

Students discuss the question in pairs. Hold a quick class vote on the most popular attraction.

Exercise 3, page 64

Play the sections one at a time. Students listen the first time for the place. Allow them to confer with a partner, check answers as a class, and repeat the section for students to make a note of any extra information. Be prepared to explain / translate: *calm* (quiet), *a tomb, a playground, a ride* (at an amusement park). Feed back as a class.

> 1 The Taj Mahal. It's calm and peaceful, one of the seven wonders of the world, 22 years to build, 20,000 workmen, completed in 1648.
> 2 Walt Disney World. It's best to stay on the site, recommends Sequoia Lodge where there's a souvenir shop, a playground, a free minibus service to the resort.
> 3 Niagara Falls. Open 24 hours a day all year round, parks are free, May to September there's a charge for parking your car, May to October there are boat rides for which it is a good idea to wear a raincoat.

Exercise 4, page 64

Students work in pairs, using a monolingual dictionary to help categorise the words. Circulate and supply vocabulary. Feed back on the answers and the additional words. The pronunciation of the following words may need particular attention: castle /ˈkɑːsəl/ (silent *t*), mosque /mɒsk/.

> • Religious buildings: cathedral, mosque, temple
> • Historic buildings: castle, palace, tower
> • Places of natural beauty: canyon, glacier, gorge

Workbook: Places to visit, page 67, exercise 8.

Exercise 5, page 65

In pairs, students make a list of the tourist attractions in their city or region. Write the following on the board:

How would you describe the place?
What is the history of the place?
What can you do there?
Is there anything you particularly recommend?

Circulate and supply vocabulary. Depending on the size of the class, each student either presents one of their ideas to a group of 6–8 students or to the class. If possible, each student should talk about a different attraction. Encourage listening students to contribute any further information about the attraction that they know. During the presentations, make a note of errors / useful language and go through these with the class at the end.

Extra Activity

If you are short of time, elicit a list of local tourist attractions on the board. Each pair then chooses a different one to prepare and present to the class.

Exercise 6, page 65

Fact File

A *stately home* is a large old house which usually has beautiful furniture, decorations and gardens. Many of these places in the UK are now owned by the government or by a preservation organisation.

Students work in pairs. Encourage them to complete as much as possible of the exercise before resorting to a monolingual dictionary. Fast finishers can underline the stressed syllable of the words or phrases.

1 b 2 e 3 g 4 a 5 f 6 d 7 h 8 c

Workbook: Places to see, page 39, exercise 1 and Describing natural features, page 67, exercise 9.

Exercise 7, page 65
Demonstrate and chorally drill the pronunciation of the three sounds. Elicit / Provide an example word for each sound, e.g. /æ/ hat, /ə/ hotter, /eɪ/ say. Students predict the pronunciation of the words before listening to check. Monitor the pronunciation as the students feed back the answers.

- /æ/ canyon, palace, valley,
- /ə/ cathedral, festival, monastery
- /eɪ/ stately home, volcano

Extra Activity
Students give examples of places like these from their own country or famous examples from abroad. They discuss which they have visited / would like to visit / are not interested in visiting and explain. Monitor pronunciation during the discussion.

Workbook: /æ/, /ə/, /eɪ/ sounds, page 40, exercise 3.

Exercise 8, page 65
Focus students' attention on the pictures and elicit the different kinds of traveller they depict. Elicit / Teach: *a backpacker, retired*. Students discuss the question in pairs or small groups. Encourage them to justify their ideas.

Exercise 9, page 66
Tell students that they are going to read about some attractions in Dublin. Ask students what they know about Dublin. Check the vocabulary in the questions: *crafts* (decorative objects made by hand), *to cater for* (to provide what somebody needs or wants), *to enable, built on an earlier site*. Set a time limit of two minutes for students to find the answers in the text. Get students to compare in pairs, indicating the words which led them to the answer.

1 Dublinia
2 Powerscourt Townhouse
3 Dublin Castle
4 Dublinia
5 Dublinia
6 Christ Church Cathedral (a mummified cat and rat)
7 Temple Bar, The Long Hall and Powerscourt Townhouse
8 Christ Church Cathedral

Exercise 10, page 66
Ask students which of the places in the box they are familiar with from the tour guide (Dublinia). Pause the recording after each conversation for students to compare their ideas with a partner. Replay any section that the students are unsure about / have misheard. Feed back briefly.

1 Want something suitable for children. Recommended: the zoo in Phoenix Park and Dublinia.
2 Want to see something outside town. Recommended: Newgrange.
3 Interested in Irish literature. Recommended: the Dublin Writer's Museum in Parnell Square.
4 Want to go to a traditional Irish pub with traditional music. Recommended: O'Donoghue's.

Exercise 11, page 67
Students discuss what they can remember about the directions to the places, before listening again. Pause and check answers after each conversation.

1 The zoo is in Phoenix Park, it is about 3 km from the city centre. To get to Dublinia, walk along Dame Street and it's behind the cathedral.
2 Take the N2 road heading north out of Dublin towards a town called Slane in County Meath. Turn right about 2 miles south of Slane and the visitor centre is signposted from there.
3 Go over Grattan Bridge at the end of Parliament Street, go up Capel Street to the end and fork right into Bolton Street. Take the third on the right into Granby Row and it's on the left, opposite the Museum of Modern Art.
4 Directions not given. It's in Merrion Row, in square E5 on the map, between St Stephen's Green and Baggott Street.

Extra Activity
- Students choose one of the conversations and practise it, using the tapescript on page 137 of the Students' Book. Monitor pronunciation and intonation.
- Students use their listening answers to improvise one of the conversations.
- Students find and underline in the tapescript expressions used for recommending and responding to recommendations.

Professional practice, page 67

Go through the phrases with the class. Point out that some are followed by the base form of the verb and others by the gerund. Elicit how you could respond to the recommendations (*What / Where / How ...? Thanks, I'll give it a try / You've been very helpful / I'll go there this evening*). Get the students to practise saying and responding to the phrases with a partner. Monitor pronunciation and intonation.

Exercise 12, page 67

Give student *A* a couple of minutes to think about what kind of things they would like to do and see. They could also check the tapescript of the listening exercise 10 for how to ask for a recommendation. Student *B* could refer back to the list of local attractions from exercise 5. Remind them to use the language for making recommendations. Student *A* starts the conversation. The conversation should only last about 1–2 minutes. Monitor and make a note of errors / useful language. Go through with the class before getting students to reverse roles.

Extra Activity

Students use the internet to research the tourist attractions of a different place.
They then role-play a tourist and a tourist information agent as above. The advantage of this role-play is that the 'tourist' genuinely doesn't know about the tourist attractions on offer.

Exercise 13, page 68

Fact File

One of the things Ireland is famous for is its traditional drink, Guinness. It's a black beer with a distinctive malty flavour and smooth, creamy head.

Ask students if they have heard of / tried Guinness. If necessary, explain what it is. Translate the list of ingredients into the students' L1 (in a monolingual class) or ask them to look the words up in a dictionary (in a multilingual class). Play the first section of the listening to 'mountains to the east'. Feed back briefly.

barley, hops, yeast, water

Exercise 14, page 68

Tell students that all of the words are verbs related to the process of making Guinness. In pairs, students match the words and definitions using a dictionary. It would also be useful at this point for students to check which of the

verbs have irregular past participles (*fed, ground*). Fast finishers discuss which of the ingredients you could boil, pump, grind, etc. Feed back briefly.

1 b 2 d 3 f 4 c 5 a 6 e

Exercise 15, page 68

Fact File

In the listening text it refers to *the wort*. This is the name for the dark, sweet liquid produced in the kieve.

Give students a couple of minutes to study the diagram and predict what is added at the different stages. Explain to students that *grist* refers to the substance produced in the grist mill. Elicit / Teach parts of the machinery: *pipe, cylinder* (where yeast is added), *storage tank*. Play the rest of the listening for students to complete the diagram.

1 is ground **2** is fed **3** mixed **4** is produced **5** are added **6** is boiled **7** is strained **8** is added **9** is fermented **10** is removed **11** is stored **12** is pumped

Language focus, page 68

Students read the language focus. Elicit the tenses of the four examples (past simple passive, gerund passive, present simple passive, modal passive). It is worth pointing out that the form of the passive is completely regular. Point out the formation of negatives and questions, particularly with the modal passive, where the students have two auxiliary verbs to manipulate.

Extra Activity

With a less confident group, elicit and write on the board the forms of the passive:

present simple	is / are	
present continuous	is / are being	
present perfect	have / has been	
past simple	was / were	+ past
future simple	will be	participle
gerund	being	
modal	must / can / should be	

Workbook: Passive, page 42, exercise 6.

Exercise 16, page 69

In pairs, students complete the sentences. If students are finding the exercise difficult, play the section of the listening which describes the process again.

1 is ground 2 is fed; is mixed 3 is produced
4 are added 5 is boiled 6 is strained, is added
7 is removed 8 is pumped, is sold

Exercise 17, page 69

Tell students they are now going to read about the wine-making process. Ask students what they know about this: *What is wine made from? When are the grapes harvested?* etc. Use this discussion and the picture to pre-teach: *grapes, to harvest, to crush, a vat, a barrel, to filter*. Ask students to read the description quickly, not worrying about the spaces, to see if there are any parts of the process they have not mentioned / did not know about. Feed back on this and any further vocabulary queries. Point out that the verb may be any form of the active or passive. Students work in pairs before checking answers with the whole class.

1 are made 2 occur 3 is (being) produced 4 are harvested 5 depends 6 take place 7 be measured
8 are crushed 9 takes place 10 lasts 11 is then stored
12 being bottled 13 filtered 14 is bottled
15 labelled 16 being released

Exercise 18, page 69

Put students in groups of three or four. Students decide what process they are going to describe. Be ready with some suggestions for groups which are short of ideas: local food and drink is a good idea. Be aware that describing a work procedure will probably only take the students ten minutes to prepare, while describing the production of a food or drink will take considerably longer, particularly if it needs researching and the students wish to have visual aids. It is therefore probably best if the whole class works on the same type of presentation. However, it will be more interesting if they choose different topics within this.

Students could research the production of a particular food or drink on the internet by using a search engine, such as yahoo.com or excite.com and looking for 'production of (name of food or drink)'. They could also print off some illustrations for their presentation.

During the preparation stage, circulate and monitor, supplying vocabulary where necessary. Point out that students do not need to script the entire presentation, but that every student should take notes so that the group can be divided and each student can give the presentation independently. The presentation should only be 2–5 minutes long. Fast finishers can practise delivering their presentation and work on visual aids.

Depending on the size of the class, students give their presentation in groups of 6–8 or to the entire class. Encourage the listeners to ask further questions. You could use this to revise indirect questions: *Do you know ...?* Feed back briefly at the end on which presentation the students learnt most from and which had the best visual aids.

Extra Activity
- Alternatively, students read their descriptions without saying what they are referring to. The listeners must identify the process they are describing as quickly as possible.
- Students write up the description of the production of a food or drink for a travel guide or as an information leaflet for the place of production.

Exercise 19 , page 70

Students discuss the questions in pairs. Feed back briefly on which museum they think is the best and why.

Exercise 20, page 70

Focus students' attention on the pictures and ask them what they can see. Tell students they are going to listen to a tour guide introducing the museum. Ask *What do you think she will talk about?* Students read the extract quickly to check their ideas (the design of the building, what you can see in the museum, other facilities). Check students understand the meaning of: *iron, a framework* (basic structure), *a sculpture, a host of* (large number of), *an exhibit, an earthquake, a volcano, a gift shop*. Point out that the spaces may be completed with more than one word. Students predict the answers before listening to check. Students compare in pairs. Feed back as a class.

1 19th-century 2 steel 3 animals 4 dinosaurs
5 displays 6 Earth galleries 7 free 8 cafeteria

Extra Activity
With a stronger class, students listen rather than read to answer the gist question *What does she talk about?* They then look at the gapped tapescript on students' book page 70, predict / recall the words in the spaces and listen again to check.

Professional practice, page 70

Check words: *a feature* (important part). Students use the extract to complete the phrases. Do the first one with the class as an example. When checking the answers, ask students to read aloud all the phrases for each category so you can check pronunciation.

1 standing outside the …
2 was designed by …
3 cafeteria, a bookshop and a gift shop
4 is free
5 one of the finest

Exercise 21, page 71

Ask students *Where can you see an exhibition?* In addition to a museum or gallery, students may provide other ideas, e.g., a civic centre, an artist's studio, etc. Students work in pairs or small groups. Give each group a monolingual dictionary to help them complete the exercise. Point out that they need to add two more words to each list. Feed back as a class. The pronunciation of the following words may need particular attention: exhibition /ˌeksəˈbɪʃən/, armour /ˈɑːmə/, landscape /ˈlændskeɪp/, statues /ˈstætʃuːz/.

- museum: armour, arrowheads, pottery, shields
  Possible extras: jewellery, ceramics, metalwork, coins and banknotes, firearms, textiles and costumes
- gallery: landscapes, canvas, sketches, statues, watercolours, portraits
  Possible extras: oil paintings, still life, a masterpiece

Workbook: Exhibitions, page 40, exercise 2.

Exercise 22, page 71

Tell students that they are going to role-play being tour guides for two London attractions, the Tower of London and Buckingham Palace. Ask students what they know about these places.

Refer students to pages 71 and 113 of the Students' Book. Students *A* work together in small groups. Allow students ten minutes to read about the Tower of London and check unknown words together, using the pictures and a monolingual dictionary to help. Students *B* do the same

for Buckingham Palace. Give students a further ten minutes to organise the information into brief presentation notes (to avoid simply reading the text), including any suitable phrases from the Professional practice box on Students' Book page 70. It is important that students practise delivering this presentation as it needs to be reasonably slow and clear, with appropriate stress and pausing. Pair off *A*s and *B*s. If there is enough room in the classroom, they should both stand at some distance from each other, encouraging the tour guide to project their voice. Explain that every tourist should have at least one question for the tour guide. Circulate and monitor, making a note of useful language / errors. Feed back briefly on which place they would prefer to visit and why, before analysing / correcting the language used.

Exercise 23, page 71

The timing of this activity depends a lot on whether students research their sight or not. If they do, and this is included in class time, it could take 60 minutes or more. If they don't, it will probably take about 40 minutes. Depending on the size of your class, you may choose to do some of the final presentations on a different day to avoid too much repetition.

Students work in pairs or small groups. They either need to choose a sight that they know a lot about, or they need to research the sight on the internet. Use a search engine, such as yahoo.com or excite.com, and search for the name of the attraction. They could also print off some visual aids from the website. The activity works better if each group chooses a different sight.

Tell students that the presentation should be at least the same length as the ones for the Tower of London and Buckingham Palace. Students decide on the information that they want to include and the order in which they are going to present it. They then review their notes on language use from the previous exercise and the language in the Professional practice box on Students' Book page 70 and discuss how they can use these. Finally, give the students five minutes to practise their presentations.

Regroup the students for the presentations. Ideally, the tour guide should stand to give their presentation, encouraging them to project their voice. Tell the tourists that they should each have at least one question to ask the tour guide at the end. Circulate and monitor during the presentations. Feed back briefly on which presentation was the most interesting and why.

Consolidation 2

For revision purposes, review the language area with the students first and then allow the students to work together in completing the exercises. Feed back as a class, asking for justification of the answers where appropriate.

For testing purposes, set a time limit for students to do one or more of the exercises individually in class. Alternatively, set the exercises as homework. If you choose to use these exercises for testing, it is worth first discussing with the students the best approach to each exercise, in particular, reading a text to understand its overall meaning before attempting to complete the gaps. Take the answers in to correct or provide the students with the answers to correct each other's.

You may also wish to evaluate students' progress in communicative performance. To do this, repeat one of the speaking / writing activities from the first four units.

Exercise 1, page 72

Review the rules on the definite and indefinite article. Ask students *How can customer loyalty be encouraged?* Elicit their ideas. Students read the text and say if it mentions anything different. Students complete the text. Refer to the Language focus box on Students' Book page 42 and the Grammar reference section on page 126.

> 1 The 2 ø 3 the 4 ø 5 ø 6 ø 7 ø 8 ø 9 a 10 ø 11 an

Exercise 2, page 72

Review the future forms and uses. Refer to the Language focus box on page 50 of the Students' Book and the Grammar reference section on page 126.

> 1 is going to 2 I'll check 3 starts 4 'm going 5 'll
> 6 leaves 7 I'll 8 are doing

Exercise 3, page 72

Check students understand the meaning of the six reporting verbs. Review the structures which follow the six verbs: infinitive, gerund, *that* + clause. Get students to match the verbs to a sentence first and then transform the sentences. Refer to the Language focus box on page 60 of the Students' Book and the Grammar reference section on page 127.

> 1 He / She promised to put the tickets in the post straightaway.
> 2 He / She refused to do any more overtime.

> 3 He / She warned me that if I didn't hurry, I'd miss my train.
> 4 He / She suggested hiring a car.
> 5 I informed him that there was a message.
> 6 I instructed her to clean the room again.

Exercise 4, page 73

Tell students to organise the vocabulary that they are sure about first and come back to those they don't remember later. There should be three words / phrases per category.

transport	luxury coach, transfer, scheduled flight
complaints	mix-up, apologise, see to something
payment	charge, company account, settle the bill
equipment	overhead projector, screen, flip chart
sightseeing	arts and crafts, historic monument, souvenirs
messages	while you were out, pass on, abbreviations

Exercise 5, page 73

Allow students to refer to the extract from the Madrid city guide on pages 52–3 of the Students' Book. Remind them to use appropriate language for making suggestions, as on page 67 of the Students' Book. Set a time limit of 30 minutes and a word count of between 100 and 130 words. Fast finishers could repeat the speaking activity, exercise 12, on page 67 of the Students' Book.

> **Suggested answer**
>
> Dear Mr Williams
>
> There is a large variety of things to do and see in Madrid. If you are interested in art, I recommend visiting the Prado Museum, which contains the finest collection of Spanish painting in the world.
>
> You might also like to think about going to the Royal Palace. If you want to go shopping, go to El Rastro. However, if I were you I'd get there early because it gets very crowded in the afternoon.
>
> In the evening, I suggest going to Casa Patas to see a flamenco show. Finally, why don't you spend one day outside Madrid, in Toledo, a Roman fortress that can be explored on foot?
>
> I hope you enjoy your stay.
>
> Best wishes

⑨ Getting around

UNIT OBJECTIVES

Professional practice:	Give advice on driving
	Give underground directions
	Car hire bookings
	Hire a motorhome
Language focus:	Modal verbs
Vocabulary:	Checking-in, using a dictionary

Unit Notes

Exercise 1, page 74

Focus students' attention on the title of the unit and ask what it means (travelling to and from different places). Students look at the picture and describe what they can see. Discuss the question with the class, supplying vocabulary where necessary, e.g., *get stuck in a traffic jam, to break down, suffer from travel / sea sickness, be delayed, be cancelled, be overbooked.*

Exercise 2, page 74

Students ask and answer the questions in pairs. If they have never had a problem themselves, suggest that they talk about someone they know who has. Monitor and supply vocabulary where necessary, e.g. *catch / miss a plane, to upgrade someone to business class, be offered compensation, be offered a complimentary drink / meal, wait in the airport terminal / departure lounge.* Feed back briefly on whose story is the most dramatic.

Exercise 3, page 74

Check students understand the five possible problems. Play the recording straight through. Students compare their ideas in pairs before checking the answer as a class. Ask students what the least serious problem is (baggage).

Fact File

Luggage and *baggage* refer to the same thing: all the cases and bags you take with you when you travel. *Luggage* is UK English, *baggage* is US English.

overbooking

Extra Activity

With less confident students, before playing the recording explain that there are two problems and they need to identify the main one.

Exercise 4, page 74

In pairs, students complete the answers they know. Play the cassette again, pausing to give students time to note and compare answers. Monitor, and replay and explain any sections that students have not understood or misunderstood.

1 18 kg.
2 There's paperwork in it that he needs on the plane.
3 He takes some things out.
4 He has an important meeting in Berlin which he can't miss.
5 No, all airlines follow the same policy.
6 Wait until 8.30 to see if he can get on this flight. If not, he will be put on the next flight.
7 She's responsible for this flight and will call the supervisor to look after people who have to wait for the next one.
8 Keep it. If they can put him on this flight, they'll take it back. If not, he'll have to check it in again.

Extra Activity

Reported speech review. Ask students to summarise the conversation using reported speech. Give them the following prompts:
She told him ... (hand baggage)
She suggested ... (take out)
She then said ... (overbooked)
He said ... (meeting)
She explained ... (wait)
He said ... (not happy)

Exercise 5, page 74

Students work individually or in pairs. Check the answers and the meaning of each one as a class. Make sure students understand the difference between a *luggage tag* and a *luggage ticket.*

Fact File

A *standby ticket* is a cheap ticket sold just before the flight if there is a seat available.

1 b 2 d 3 e 4 a 5 f 6 c

Workbook: Vocabulary, page 44, exercise 1.

Exercise 6, page 75
Explain that the six words are similar in meaning but used differently. Encourage students to read all the definitions before working with a partner to insert the words. Check these answers as a class. The pronunciation of the following words may need particular attention: journey /ˈdʒɜːni/, tour /tʊə/, voyage /ˈvɔɪ-ɪdʒ/. Students then complete the sentences below and compare with a partner. Monitor and only feed back if necessary.

1 journey 2 trip 3 tour 4 crossing 5 voyage
6 excursion
1 journey 2 crossing 3 voyage 4 trip 5 tour
6 excursion

Extra Activity
In pairs, students discuss which of the above they have done. Demonstrate by talking about one or two of your experiences first.

Workbook: Vocabulary, page 44, exercise 2.

Exercise 7, page 75
Check words: *to ensure* (make certain), *to go to plan* (happen as organised). Students discuss the question in pairs. Circulate and supply vocabulary. Feed back briefly on their ideas for ensuring that a journey goes to plan.

Exercise 8, page 76
Focus students' attention on the information leaflet and ask them what it is about (passport and visa rules). Students read the six statements and discuss in pairs whether they think they are true or false. Be prepared to explain / translate: *over, a criminal record, be allowed to*. Set a time limit of three minutes for students to find the answers in the information leaflet. In order for students to answer the questions they will need to understand: *be required to* (must), *a waiver* (an official written statement saying that a rule can be ignored). Students compare in pairs before checking their answers as a class.

1 F Children who are 16 and under and are included on a parent's passport at the time of the change in law do not need their own passport.
2 F Children over 16 must have their own passport.
3 T (assuming a holiday is normally less than 90 days)
4 F They may be allowed to enter – they need to make a visa application in advance.
5 T
6 T

Language focus, page 76
Students find and underline all the verbs in the information leaflet. Encourage students to use these examples to help complete the table.

Extra Activity
Students compare in pairs before checking as a class. Highlight:
* verbs that can be contracted (*can't, don't have to, mustn't*)
* the use of the bare infinitive after *can, must* and *should*
* verbs in the passive which need the verb *to be* (*be required to, be allowed to, be authorised to*)
* the difference in meaning between *must not* (there is an obligation not to do something) and *do not have to* (it is not necessary to do this)
* *may* has two possible uses, giving permission (*children may continue to travel ...*) and indicating a possibility (*entry may be denied ...*) The use will be clear from the context.
* the same meaning can be expressed with different verbs, e.g. *must, have to* and *be required to* all express obligation
* some of the verbs are more formal and are usually only used in official documents (*may* [for permission], *be required to, be authorised to* and uncontracted forms, e.g., *cannot, must not, do not have to*)

	giving permission	refusing permission	expressing obligation	expressing no obligation	giving advice	indicating a possibility
have to			✓			
be required to			✓			
may	✓					✓
can	✓					
cannot		✓				
be allowed to	✓					
should					✓	
do not have to					✓	
must not		✓				
be authorised to	✓					
must			✓			

Extra Activity

Students discuss the rules and regulations:
– for entering their country
– if they want to travel to the US
– if they want to travel in Europe

Exercise 9, page 77

Tell students that they are going to read about the rules and regulations of driving in New York. Ask students to predict what the article will say about renting a car and parking. Students work in pairs to complete the text. Encourage them to work out unknown words from the context but be prepared to explain / translate: *to take out* (to arrange to get something officially), *damage and liability protection* (insurance against legal responsibility to pay money for damage and injury), *vandalism*, *gas(oline)* (US English: *petrol* in UK English), *curb* (US English: *kerb* in UK English). Circulate, pointing out if necessary that:

– *will must* is not possible, the future is *will have to*
– the verb *to be* at the beginning of a space is a clue
– *may well* is an expression meaning *is more than possible*

Check the answers as a class.

> **1** don't have to **2** must **3** required to **4** have to
> **5** should **6** have to **7** may **8** must not **9** authorised to
> **10** must

Extra Activity

With a less confident class, books closed, students predict what the article will say is an obligation and what it will recommend. Students make two columns in their notebooks: *obligation* and *recommendation*. Read the completed text to the students, slowly and clearly and ask students to note down obligations and recommendations (some parts of the text are neither and they should ignore these). Students compare notes and then check as a class. They then open their books and attempt to complete the text, having already heard it once and knowing the meaning of most of the sentences.

Workbook: Modal verbs, page 45, exercise 5.

Exercise 10, page 77

This exercise introduces two further modal auxiliary verbs, *needn't* and *might*, and the use of *must, should, can* and *can't* for possibility. If students are still struggling to understand the uses of the modal auxiliary verbs presented in the Language focus on page 76, omit this exercise and move on to the speaking practice. With more confident students, get them to work in pairs. Be prepared to explain / translate: *hurry, obey*. Check the answers as a class. Point out the meaning of the modal auxiliary verbs in this exercise.

> **1** b (needn't = don't have to)
> **2** f
> **3** h
> **4** d (might = possibility)
> **5** a (must = is logically certain)
> **6** g (can't = is logically impossible)
> **7** e (can = theoretical possibility)
> **8** c (should = strong probability)

Workbook: Signs, page 44, exercise 3.

Exercise 11, page 77

Check words: *tips* (advice). In pairs, students discuss the advice they would give. Students could then change partners and compare their ideas. Feed back on what is the most important piece of advice in each area.

Travel guide project

Students write an information leaflet for visitors planning to rent a car / drive in their country.

Exercise 12, page 78

Tell students that they are now going to hear about transport in Sydney. Ask students what they know about Sydney. Students read the four questions. Check words: *to head for*. Play the conversations one at a time, pausing to allow students to compare their answers. Replay any sections which the students have not understood or misunderstood.

1 because she thinks she should know the answer
2 the Opera House
3 a newsagent's
4 once

Extra Activity
With conversations 1 and 3, pause after the first speaker and get students to predict the second speaker's response.

Exercise 13, page 78

Check words: *to overtake*. In pairs, students use the prompts to try to reconstruct the conversations orally. Play the conversations again, pausing between each one to give students time to make a note of useful language. Students then reconstruct the four conversations. Emphasise that they need to express the same meaning as the original conversation, but don't necessarily need to use the same words. Circulate and monitor, correcting as necessary. Students practise their conversations in pairs. After reversing roles, encourage students to go back to the prompts in the students' book and repeat the role-play using only these.

Extra Activity
Students compare their versions with the tapescript on page 139 of the Students' Book. Discuss whether the language differences are equally acceptable or not.

Exercise 14, page 78

Give students one minute to study the phrases for using the underground. Elicit what type of words go in the spaces, e.g., *get on the train at* (name of station), *you want the* (colour / name of line) *line travelling in the direction of* (final stop in that direction), *get off at* (name of station / the nth stop), etc. You may also wish to teach your students *the ... line travelling south / north / east / west*. Elicit the question: *Can you tell me the way to ... / how to get to ... by underground?* Refer students to the appropriate pages and give them time to study the map of Sydney CityRail. Point out that they should always start from Central Station. If necessary, ask two strong students to

demonstrate the activity. Circulate and monitor. Get students to check their completed maps with each other at the end.

Tips: During an information gap speaking activity, make sure that students cannot read their partner's information. One way to do this is to have the students sitting at a distance from each other. This has the added advantage of making monitoring easier.

Extra Activity
• Elicit how the language would be different if you were giving directions by bus, e.g. *get on the bus in front of the shopping centre in ... street, you want the 327 bus travelling in the direction of ...*, etc.
• Test students' knowledge of their local transport system by asking *What's the quickest way to get to ...?* This can be done as a class or as a team competition.
• Photocopy or bring in a local bus or underground map. Give students a starting point, e.g. you are at the tourist information office. Students role-play a tourist and a tourist information agent or passer-by. The tourist asks how to get to different sights around town.

Exercise 15, page 78

Students ask and answer the questions in pairs. Circulate and monitor, supplying vocabulary where necessary, e.g., *a one-day travelcard, a bus / an underground pass for ten journeys.*

Exercise 16, page 79

Tell students they are going to read about getting around Sydney. Give them one minute to scan the text for all the different types of transport mentioned (foot, bus, train, underground, light railway, passenger ferry, taxi boat). In pairs, students then read the text in more detail and insert the prepositions. Be prepared to explain / translate: *coupled with* (together with), *harbourside suburbs, be purchased, on board, a train carriage, a wharf* (a platform made of stone or wood at the side of a river where ships and boats can be tied up), *to pick someone up, to drop someone off*. Check answers as a class.

1 on 2 within 3 in 4 between 5 on 6 from 7 into 8 on 9 at / in 10 inside 11 through 12 at 13 at 14 to 15 from 16 around 17 up 18 off

Travel guide project

Students write a similar text for getting around their own town or city.

Workbook: Compound nouns, page 45, exercise 4 and Prepositions, page 48, exercise 8.

Exercise 17, page 79

Check students understand the meaning of: *barrier, pier* (jetty), *via* (going through a place, e.g. *We flew from London to Sydney via Bangkok*). In pairs, students predict whether the underlined letters in the two words have the same sound. Play the cassette / CD, pausing after each pair for students to check their answers. In pairs, students practise saying the words.

1 ✗ 2 ✗ 3 ✗ 4 ✓ 5 ✗ 6 ✗ 7 ✗ 8 ✓

P Photocopiable extra, see pages 86–87
Getting around Sydney
You will need one copy of plan A and one of plan B for each pair of students.

Language: asking for and giving directions

- Put students into pairs and give one student a copy of plan A and one student a copy of plan B. Allow them a minute or two to read the information. Remind students of the further useful language in the professional practice box on Students' Book page 78.

- Students work in pairs, asking for and giving directions to the different places. Make sure that students cannot read their partner's information. One way to do this is to have the students sitting at a distance from each other. This has the added advantage of making monitoring easier. The aim is for students to accurately complete their map of Sydney.

- When they have finished, students compare their plans to see if they have correctly located the places.

Exercise 18, page 80

In pairs, students discuss the questions. Feed back on the type of documents the car hire company can ask for, e.g. *a printout of the rental agreement* (if booked over the internet), *valid driving licences for all named drivers, passport or identity card, proof of address* (a recent addressed envelope), *the credit card being used for additional expenses.*

Exercise 19, page 80

Fact File

- A *Collision Damage Waiver* covers you for damage you may cause to the rented vehicle. In order to be insured against damage you cause to other people and property you need to take out *Third Party Liability / Cover*.
- A *booster* is a removable extra seat put onto a car seat for a child to sit in order to make the child high enough for the safety belt to fit safely.

Check students understand the vocabulary in the questions: *low / high season, to break down.* Set a time limit of three minutes for students to find the answers in the car hire form. Students compare in pairs before checking answers as a class.

1 $386 (7 x $38 + 3 x $40)
2 Toyota Tarago
3 $5 per day
4 Holden Commodore and Toyota Tarago
5 $812
6 $252 (4 x [$44 + $9 (peak period surcharge) + $10 (CDW)]
7 There is 24-hour emergency roadside assistance
8 Refill the tank

Exercise 20, page 81

Focus students' attention on the car hire booking form. Give students one minute to check the information they are listening for. Make sure students understand that *pax* means passengers. Warn students that they will not hear the information in the same order as it is on the form. Play the cassette / CD, pausing after 2–3 questions have been answered for students to compare their answers in pairs. Replay any sections that the students have missed or misunderstood.

1 Dumas 2 Annette 3 Mrs 4 Yes 5 Nissan Pulsar
6 international 7 Yes 8 4 9 Yes 10 CDW 11 21/3
12 25/3 13 Mastercard

Professional practice, page 81

Students read the Professional practice box and predict how the phrases are completed. Play the recording again, pausing after each phrase is said to confirm that students have heard it correctly. Feed back also on any acceptable alternatives the students had, e.g. *Would you like the unlimited distance option?* Ask students why the future continuous is used in questions 5 and 6 (see unit 6: to ask questions about future plans politely). Practise the phrases by repetition drilling.

1 And how long
2 What kind of driver's licence
3 Do you want
4 Do you want the
5 you'll be dropping it off
6 How will you be paying

Extra Activity

Role-play. Students use the completed booking form to role-play the conversation between Kiwi Motorhomes and Annette Dumas. Alternatively, use a blank booking form from the internet. Some hire company websites display the whole page, e.g., www.hertz.com. Most take you through a step-by-step process, so you will need several pages. Students can then improvise their booking details.

Exercise 21, page 81

This activity should take about ten minutes preparation and 5–10 minutes to carry out the role-play.

Focus students' attention on the picture of the motorhome. Elicit / Teach *motorhome* and ask students *How is a motorhome different from a car?* Explain that, depending on how many people can sleep in the motorhome, it is called a 2 / 4 / 6 *berth* motorhome.

Divide students into *A* and *B* and explain their roles. Refer them to the appropriate page and allow them ten minutes preparation time.

Students *A* work together in pairs / small groups. Read through the information about Kiwi Motorhomes on page 118 of the Students' Book, checking vocabulary with each other. Check students' comprehension of key points by asking or giving the students the following questions: *What features does the motorhome have which makes it like a home? When is it cheapest to hire a motorhome? Is that the rate per day? Does that include insurance? Does the customer need to pay a deposit? What happens if they cancel?*

Students *B* work together in pairs / small groups. They prepare the questions they need to ask in order to get the information listed. Monitor, reminding them to use indirect questions occasionally (*Could you tell me ...?*). They should also consider further questions they could ask. Point out that in reality they would probably phone several companies to compare terms and conditions so they should make a note of *A*'s answers.

Pair off students *A* and *B*. Student *B* should start the conversation with Kiwi Motorhomes: *How can I help you?* Circulate and monitor, making a note of useful language / errors for correction and analysis later.

Fast finishers should continue on with the conversation, with Student *A* taking the booking. Feed back briefly on whether Student *B* thinks it is a good deal and whether the students would like to travel around in a motorhome for a couple of weeks.

Tips: To role-play telephone conversations, have students sitting back-to-back. That way, as in a real telephone conversation, they cannot use any visual clues. It also means that students have to speak louder and it is easier to monitor language problems.

Extra Activity

Students reverse roles. Student *B* studies car and cost information from a different car hire company, e.g., www.alamo.com, www.hertz.com or www.avis.com. Student *A* decides the details of their holiday and thinks about any questions they want to ask. They role-play the telephone call as above.

---

⑩ Eating out

UNIT OBJECTIVES

Professional practice:	Describe dishes
	Recommend a restaurant
	Prepare a menu
	Take an order
Language focus:	Countable and uncountable nouns, quantifiers
Vocabulary:	Verbs of food preparation

Unit Notes

Exercise 1, page 82

Focus students' attention on the pictures and ask them to describe what they can see. Elicit / Teach the word *snails*. Students discuss the questions in pairs.

Exercise 2, page 82

Set a time limit of two minutes for students to match the headings with paragraphs. Emphasise that they only need to understand the topic of each paragraph and that they should not worry about unknown words at this point. Students compare their answers in pairs before checking as a class.

> **1** f **2** d **3** a **4** e **5** c

Exercise 3, page 82

Check words: *spicy*. Students read the statements and predict the answers. Give students a further five minutes to read the text in more detail. Encourage students to guess the meaning of new words from the context. Students compare their answers in pairs before checking as a class.

> **1** T
> **2** F It tends not to be highly spiced.
> **3** F Spirits are generally not drunk before a meal in France. Kir (white wine with a blackcurrant liqueur) is a typical aperitif.
> **4** T
> **5** T
> **6** F It usually carries an extra charge.
> **7** F You do not have to leave a tip but it is common to do so.

Extra Activity

Students find and underline all the food-related words in the text, e.g., in paragraph A, *meat, poultry, fish, regional, simple, fresh, seasonal, spiced, herbs, chives, parsley, sauce, savoury*. Students divide the words into categories, e.g., *meat, seafood, dairy products, herbs, adjectives*, etc. and add two more words to each list.

Exercise 4, page 83

Discuss the cuisine of the students' region / country together: *Is it changing? What is it centred on? Is it simple / spicy? Are sauces important?* Students continue discussing each section in pairs. Circulate and monitor, supplying vocabulary where necessary.

Extra Activity

If you have students from different countries in the class, get each one to do a short presentation on eating out in their country, covering the topics in the reading.

Travel guide project

Students write a description of eating out in their city or country, modelled on the reading text.

Exercise 5, page 84

Tell students that the verbs refer to ways of preparing food. Ask students if they can explain or give an example for any of them. Give students definitions for the new verbs. Students listen to the definition and suggest which verb it is. Check comprehension by asking *What type of food is baked / sliced / fried? What can you use to garnish fish?* Drill the words chorally. Students complete the exercise in pairs. Encourage them to use the pictures to help. Be prepared to explain / translate: *flaky* (consisting of many very thin layers), *pastry, a crescent, garlic, stock, scallops, pork, intestines, tarragon, tender, lamb, a cutlet*.

1 baked 2 steamed 3 sliced 4 garnished
5 grilled 6 poached 7 fried 8 served

Extra Activity
- Students copy the verbs into their notebooks with a list of two or three foodstuffs related to the verb, e.g. *baked – bread, cakes, apple, potato.*
- Elicit and add further verbs to the list, e.g. roasted, barbecued, boiled, coated, flavoured with, chilled.

Exercise 6, page 84
Students ask and answer the questions in pairs. Circulate and supply vocabulary where necessary, e.g., *I'm not keen on ..., I'm allergic to ..., that sounds tasty / disgusting.*

Exercise 7, page 85
Focus students' attention on the pictures and get them to speculate what the ingredients are. Students look at the table and the example. Be prepared to explain / translate: *wild, creamy, thick* (not flowing easily), *trout, egg custard, lidded pot, shrimp.* Give students a couple of minutes in pairs to complete the sentences. Call on individual students to read the descriptions of the dishes. Feed back briefly on which dish they would most like to try.

2 Noisettes d'agneau are small, tender lamb cutlets fried in butter and served with a variety of garnishes.
3 Chawan mushi is a thick egg custard steamed in a small lidded pot and served with vegetables, shrimp and other seafood.
4 Gefüllte Forella is wild trout steamed and served with a salad and mushrooms.

Workbook: Ways of cooking, page 50, exercise 2 and Explaining dishes, page 50, exercise 3.

Professional practice, page 85
Ask students if they know what *pollo al ajillo* is. Can they describe it? Students read the description to check.

Exercise 8, page 85
Have some suggestions ready for students who are unable to think of three examples. Encourage them to choose dishes that a foreigner really wouldn't know about rather than dishes like paella or moussaka. Give students five minutes to prepare their descriptions. Circulate and supply vocabulary. Students then read their description to a different partner, who listens and identifies the dish.

Travel guide project
Students write up their descriptions for the travel guide, including photos of the food if possible.

Language focus, page 86
Read through the rules as a class. Elicit / Suggest more examples of countable and uncountable food and drink. Point out that most uncountable nouns are singular and take the singular form of the verb, e.g. *Spaghetti is my favourite food.* Explain that many uncountable nouns become countable when we are talking about kinds or varieties of things, e.g. *Australian wines* refers to 'kinds of wine'.

Workbook: Countable and uncountable nouns, page 51, exercise 4.

Exercise 9, page 86
Check words: *lamb tikka* (mild curry dish of lamb in tomato-based sauce, very popular in the UK), *to run out of, a tie.* Students complete the exercise in pairs. Feed back as a class.

1 rice
2 bread
3 egg
4 a fly
5 delicious chicken
6 an excellent beer (one kind of beer which is excellent) / excellent beer (in general) / some excellent beers (kinds of beer)

Exercise 10, page 86
Get students to cover the words and, in pairs, see how many of the pictures they can describe, making the food countable. Give students two minutes to do the matching exercise. Fast finishers should think of other foodstuffs that could be used with these 'quantities'. Check answers as a class.

You can have a *carafe* of wine or water.
You can have a *rack* of lamb or pork: it's a large piece of meat from the side of an animal.

1 a pot of tea (a)
2 a carafe of wine (b)
3 a rack of lamb (h)
4 a bottle of mineral water (g)
5 a bunch of grapes (c)
6 a plate of snails (d)
7 a fillet of fish (f)
8 a bowl of rice (e)

Extra Activity
Pronunciation focus. Highlight and practise the linking sounds in the expressions of quantity, e.g., *a pot of* /əpɒtəf/, *a carafe of* /əkəræfəf/. Explain that we always link words where the first finishes in a consonant sound and the second starts with a vowel sound.

Exercise 11, page 87

Check students understand the meaning of: *lobster*. Write *lobster* on the board and ask students which syllable is stressed: /ˈlɒbstə/. Ask students how the unstressed syllable is pronounced. Write /tə/ above the unstressed syllable and demonstrate how it is pronounced. Write on the board: *Can I have the lobster with a green salad, please?* Ask students which words are stressed: *Can I have the lobster with a green salad, please?* Highlight the vowel sounds in the unstressed words: Can I /kənaɪ/, the /ðə/, with a /wɪðə/. Explain that the /ə/ sound is the most common vowel sound in English. It is never stressed and often found in weak forms. Students look at the words on Students' Book page 87 and predict how they are pronounced, then listen and repeat. In pairs, students mark the schwa /ə/ sounds in the sentences. If students are missing examples, tell them the number of /ə/ sounds in each sentence. Check answers as a class and then get students to practise saying the sentences in pairs.

1 Pasta gives you energy.
2 There was a lot of people at the dinner party.
3 I'd like a chocolate-flavoured ice cream.
4 What have you ordered for breakfast?
5 Can you pass me the salt and pepper, please?
6 I'd like a glass of mineral water, please.

Language focus, page 87

Read through the Language focus as a class. Highlight:

- with singular countable nouns you use *a / an*, e.g. *There is an excellent eatery. If you need an extra spoon.*

- *some* can be used in a negative sentence and *any* in a positive one. This is relatively unusual and, because of this, *some* and *any* are often stressed in this type of sentence:

I don't like some of the food they serve.
I like any fresh green vegetables.

- the difference between *few*, which emphasises the negative, meaning *not many*, and *a few* which emphasises the positive and means *some*. This is the same with *little* (not much) and *a little* (some).

- *many* and *much* are used most often in negatives and questions. In positive sentences we tend to use *lots of*, *a lot of* and *plenty of*. We use *many* and *much* in positive sentences in formal style, or with *too, so, very, as*.

Students often believe that the word *any* makes a sentence negative, e.g., They say *I like any kind of vegetable* when they mean *I don't like any kind of vegetable*. If this is a common problem among your students, use these two example sentences and ask students to contrast them. Remind students that a sentence is only negative in English if it has *not* or *no* in it.

Extra Activity
Draw a noughts and crosses grid on the board with: *some, any, much, many, no, a few, little, a lot* and *plenty of* in the squares of the grid. Divide the students into two teams. The team nominates a square and makes a sentence using the word in that square. If the sentence is accurate (and true) they win the box. Teams take it in turns. The winning team is the first to get three in a row.

Workbook: Quantifiers, page 52, exercise 6.

Exercise 12, page 87

Elicit different types of 'ethnic food' restaurants you might find in a city. Give students one minute to read the article and find the ones listed (Chinese, Algerian, Tunisian, Moroccan, Japanese, vegetarian). Check words: *be spoilt for choice* (there are so many it is difficult to choose one), *on request*. In pairs, students complete the text. Check the answers as a class.

1 many 2 many 3 little 4 a few 5 few 6 any 7 many
8 many 9 a little

Exercise 13, page 88

Focus students' attention on the three pictures. Ask students to speculate on how old they are, what they do and what type of restaurant they would go to. Give students one minute to read and recommend a restaurant. Emphasise that they do not need to understand every word. Students compare their ideas in pairs and discuss which restaurant they would go to and why.

<table>
<tr><td>none of</td><td></td></tr>
<tr><td>only one</td><td></td></tr>
<tr><td>a few</td><td></td></tr>
<tr><td>some</td><td></td></tr>
<tr><td>the majority of</td><td>restaurant(s) in (city / area) ...</td></tr>
<tr><td>all</td><td></td></tr>
<tr><td>the cheapest</td><td></td></tr>
<tr><td>the most expensive</td><td></td></tr>
</table>

none of
only one
a few
some
the majority of   *restaurant(s) in (city / area) ...*
all
the cheapest
the most expensive

Groups consider how to summarise their findings using this language. Fast finishers discuss which of the restaurants in their table they would usually eat at and why. Finally, students regroup and summarise their findings. The listeners comment on which restaurants they have eaten at / would like to eat at.

Extra Activity

Students find in the texts ways to describe:
- a restaurant, e.g., *restored, touristy*
- its food, e.g., *the menu has something for everyone, fine cuisine*
- the service, e.g., *impeccable, friendly*

Exercise 14, page 88

Ask students *What factors influence your choice of restaurant?* Students compare their ideas to the factors along the top of the table. Give students one minute to study the table. Check students' comprehension by asking *Can you eat fish at La Baracane? Can you eat outside at Le Trumilou? Which is the most expensive / the cheapest restaurant?* Explain that the tourists don't actually say the name of any restaurants, they just discuss some of the factors listed in the table. Play the recording once straight through. Students compare their ideas in pairs, explaining what they understood which led them to the answer. Play the recording again to allow them to confirm the answer.

Chez Jenny

Exercise 15, page 89

Demonstrate the activity by choosing a restaurant yourself first and getting the students to ask you questions until they are certain which restaurant it is. Students continue in pairs.

Exercise 16, page 89

Students work in small groups. They copy the table layout into their notebooks. Groups discuss what are the influencing factors when choosing a restaurant in their country and write them along the top. In addition to the ones in the example, students might consider: which credit cards are taken, whether it has a good wine list / a bar area, whether you can try a particular national cuisine there, whether it is open at lunchtime. They could do this activity based on their local knowledge. However, it works best if the restaurants are researched on the internet. You could either do this yourself and print off some restaurant information for the students, or the students could research the restaurants themselves. Set a target of eight restaurants. You may wish to ask different groups to research restaurants in different parts of the city / area as this will create more interest in each other's work. As students are finishing the table, write the following on the board:

Extra Activity
- While students are researching restaurants, they make a note of descriptive vocabulary for restaurants, the food and the service.
- Students consider which restaurant they would recommend for the different types of tourist in exercise 13 on page 88 of the Students' Book.
- Students review the language of recommendations on Students' Book page 67. They then role-play a tourist asking a tourist information agent to recommend a particular type of restaurant.

Exercise 17, page 89

Students read the questions. Play the recording, pausing to allow students to compare their answers. Replay any sections that the students have not understood / misunderstood.

1 Kir
2 Mary possibly went there for a working lunch a few years before
3 French onion soup and snails
4 because it is typically French
5 rack of lamb
6 she asks for the lamb without the mint sauce
7 Béarnaise sauce with tomato purée
8 a bottle of Cabernet Sauvignon

Professional practice, page 89

Students predict the sentences first, before listening to check. Pause after each sentence is heard for students to compare, then check as a class. Point out the use of *madam* and *sir* as polite ways of speaking to a woman and man. Drill the phrases chorally.

1 If you would like to
2 take your coat
3 Here's the
4 something to drink before your meal
5 Are you ready to
6 And what would you like
7 I'd certainly recommend
8 So that's

Workbook: Serving guests, page 52, exercise 7.

Extra Activity

Elicit the basic structure of a typical restaurant conversation on the board:

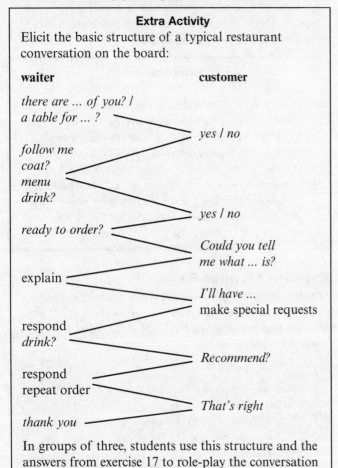

In groups of three, students use this structure and the answers from exercise 17 to role-play the conversation in the restaurant.

Exercise 18, page 89

This activity should take 30–40 minutes. Organise the students into groups of 3–4 students. Give students five minutes to discuss what they are going to include in their traditional menu. Students could either invent the menu or use / adapt a menu from a local restaurant. Most restaurants which have websites, have menus. Some have translations against which students could compare their versions at the end.

Once students know what they are going to include on the menu, give each group a bilingual dictionary to help them translate it into English. Allow 20 minutes for this stage. Refer students back to the language for describing dishes on page 85. Circulate and monitor, supplying vocabulary where necessary.

Finally, students should make one or two neat copies of the menu in preparation for the role-play. For a more authentic role-play prop, back these menus with cardboard. Fast finishers should make a note of any new related vocabulary they have needed.

Exercise 19, page 89

This speaking activity will work best if you can arrange the classroom to look more like a restaurant, with seating for 2–4 customers around tables. Students work in groups of 3–4, each student in the group having worked in a different group when preparing the menu. Each waiter needs a copy of the menu their group prepared. Point out that, unless the waiter has a very good memory, they will need to make a note of the order so that they can repeat it back to customers. Get students to role-play the conversation from the arrival of the customers. Circulate and monitor, making a note of useful language and errors. Feed back briefly on these areas before students change roles and repeat the role-play, so that students can incorporate the new language / corrections in the next round. Continue until most / all students have been the waiter once.

Extra Activity

- With a mixed ability group, give more confident students the role of waiter first. This will give less confident students a model to follow.
- Take a class vote on the best menu (students cannot vote for their own).

Traditions

Unit Notes

Exercise 1, page 90

Students discuss the questions in groups or as a class. Use the pictures to pre-teach: *a candle, to clap your hands, a cap, a bib, a stick, a jewel*.

Exercise 2, page 90

Tell students they are going to hear four people talking about the traditions in the pictures. Play the extracts one at a time, allowing students to compare their ideas in pairs, explaining what they heard which lead them to the answer. Feed back as a class.

	Tradition	Country
1	Kwanzaa festival	USA / the World
2	Jizo statues	Japan
3	Flamenco	Spain
4	The Highland Games	Scotland

Exercise 3, page 90

In pairs, students match the traditions and the categories from memory.

1 moral values 2 religion 3 artistic expression
4 sport

Exercise 4, page 91

Check words: *to light* (a candle), *heaven, respectable* (considered to be socially acceptable). In pairs, students complete the answers they know. Play the cassette again, pausing after each extract for students to compare in pairs. Replay any parts that students have missed or misunderstood.

1 F It's a celebration of family, community and
     cultural roots.
2 F One candle is lit each day.
3 F They are associated with Buddhism.
4 T
5 T
6 F A flamenco performance is improvised.
7 F *Usually* in northern Scotland.
8 T

Extra Activity
Ask students *Which of these traditions have you heard of / seen? Which would you like to see? Do you have any similar / comparable traditions?*

Workbook: Vocabulary, page 54, exercises 2 and 3.

Exercise 5, page 91

In pairs, students match the verbs and nouns that they already know. Encourage students to teach each other new vocabulary before / instead of asking you. Be prepared to explain / translate: *to decorate, to drink a toast* (an expression of good wishes or respect for someone which involves holding up and then drinking from a glass of alcohol after a short speech), *to let off fireworks, to honour* (to give public praise or reward), *a costume, a flag, a prayer, a float, a victory*.

1 b 2 d 3 h 4 f 5 c 6 i 7 e 8 j 9 g 10 a

Extra Activity
- Students work in pairs. Student *A* covers the verbs and only looks at the nouns. Student *B* reads a verb and *A* chooses the noun. Alternatively, student *A* closes their book and attempts to remember the noun, with *B* prompting where necessary. Students then reverse roles.
- In pairs, students discuss: *Which of these actions have you done? Explain the situation.*

Exercise 6, page 91

Tell students that all the words are related to traditions. Explain that the process of categorising vocabulary makes it more memorable. Provide each pair with a monolingual dictionary and give them five minutes to organise the words. Point out that the word *fast* here does not refer to speed. At the end, join pairs together to compare how they chose to categorise the words.

- ways of celebrating: parade, carnival, procession
- things you give: presents, flowers, cards
- related to the past: tradition, heritage, folklore
- related to religion: fast, pray, pilgrimage

Exercise 7, page 91

Students can work in pairs or small groups to think of examples of traditions that fit the categories. Elicit their answers and write them on the board. The class can then vote for the best example for each category. If there is enough time, ask students to explain why they voted for a particular tradition.

Exercise 8, page 92

Ask *Has anyone been to Japan? What do you know about Japanese lifestyle / food / religion / geography / traditions?* Ask if anyone knows about the tea ceremony in Japan. Can they answer any of the questions before reading the extract? Set a time limit of two minutes for students to find the answers. Encourage students to guess the meaning of unknown words from the context. Students compare their ideas with a partner before class feedback.

1 Recognition that every human encounter is a unique occasion that can, and will, never recur again exactly.
2 Meeting the guests, a purification with fresh water in a stone basin, walking through the grounds of the teahouse, watching the tea being prepared, consuming food and drinking the tea.
3 It is associated with Zen Buddhism ideals: the whole universe is experienced in the drinking of a bowl of tea by giving oneself over totally to the here and now and fully participating with a heart free from selfish desires.
4 Harmony, respect, purity and tranquillity.

Language focus, page 93

From memory, students recall the meaning of *chashitsu*, *matcha* and *Sen no Rikyu*. They check their answers with the three model sentences. Be prepared to explain / translate: *whipped, powdered, nobleman* (belonging to a high social rank). Highlight the defining relative clauses in the sentences. Go through the rules with the class. Ask: *Which relative pronoun is used for people* (who) / *things or animals* (which) / *places* (where) / *time* (when)? Point out that *who* / *which* can be replaced by *that*, and *whose* means *of who* or *of which*.

Workbook: Relative clauses, page 58, exercise 8.

Exercise 9, page 93

Write the words on the board first and ask if any of the students can define them. Students read the definitions to check their ideas. Check students understand: *a container, a puppet, a ceremony, a relic* (an object from the past which has survived), *a role* (job), *martial art, to date back*. Individually or in pairs, students complete the sentences with relative pronouns.

Fact File

The *shogun* was the hereditary commander of the Japanese army who ruled Japan.

1 which / that 2 which / that 3 which / that 4 where
5 whose 6 which / that

P Photocopiable extra, see page 88

Relative clauses crossword

You will need a copy of each crossword for each pair of students.

Language: relative clauses
vocabulary from units 9–11

- Divide students into two groups, *A* and *B*. Give a copy of Student *A* crossword to students in group *A*, and a copy of Student *B* crossword to those in group *B*.

- Students work together in their separate groups to check they know the meaning of the words in their half of the crossword. (All the vocabulary is taken from units 9–11)

- Put students in pairs so that one Student *A* and one Student *B* are working together. They are not allowed to look at each other's crossword.

- Students take it in turns to describe the words that appear on their half of the crossword to their partner, using defining relative clauses (*It's a person who ..., it's a time when you ...*, etc.) The partner has to guess the words, and write them in their own crossword.

- Students continue until they both have a completed version of the crossword.

Professional practice, page 93

Go through the explanation as a class. Check words: *matting* (strong, rough material used to cover floors). Elicit more examples using words from the students' first language (in a monolingual class) or simple English words (in a multilingual class).

Exercise 10, page 93

Draw students' attention to the pictures and ask them what they think these things are. Students check their ideas and, in pairs, make sentences describing the items using the vague language. This should be a spoken rather than a written exercise, as this is when vague language is most usual.

1 A *kimono* is a sort / kind of garment made of silk which women wear on formal occasions.
2 *Omamori* are a sort / kind of good luck charms that are related to health, safety when driving and fertility.
3 *Sushi* refers to a variety of dishes. It's a sort / kind of cold vinegared rice wrapped with raw fish.
4 *Dosojin stones* are a sort / kind of roadside stone which guard travellers and mark village boundaries.
5 *Pachinko* are a sort / kind of pinball machine without flippers and is the most popular form of entertainment in Japan.

Extra Activity

Vocabulary games

- Write vocabulary from previous classes on slips of paper. In pairs or small groups, students define the words to each other. This could be done as a competition: the first group to get ten right wins.
- Alternatively, divide the class into teams. One student from each team turns their back to the board. The rest of the team faces this team member and the board. Write a word from previous classes on the board. The team must define the word to their member. The first one to identify the word wins a point. Change the student who is guessing the word and continue.

Exercise 11, page 94

Tell students that they are going to listen to a description of traditional Japanese theatre. Students match the theatre vocabulary to the definitions. Students work in pairs. Encourage them to complete what they already know first and then finish the exercise together as a class. The pronunciation of the following words may need particular attention: cast /kɑːst/, characters /ˈkærɪktəz/.

1 b 2 f 3 e 4 d 5 c 6 a

Workbook: The theatre, page 58, exercise 9.

Exercise 12, page 94

Students read the introduction. Check words: *lobby* (the room into which the main entrance door opens). Use the pictures to revise the word *puppet*. Check students understand the type of information they need to write under each heading. Tell students that some information is not in the listening. The listening is in three sections. Pause after each section for students to compare their ideas. Play the section again for students to complete their notes. Replay any parts that the students have not heard or have misunderstood. Get the students to check their answers against the tapescript, Students' Book page 141.

	Noh	Kabuki	Bunraku
Origins	14th century	17th century	early 17th century
Audience	higher social classes	ordinary people	n/a
Themes	gods, warriors, beautiful women and supernatural beings	historical events and relationships between men and women	historical events and relationships between men and women
Costume	masks	elaborate, exaggerated make-up	puppets, the puppeteer wears traditional formal dress
Stage	outdoor wooden stage	well-equipped wooden stage with trapdoors and footbridge	n/a
Music	traditional drums and flutes	n/a	traditional music performed on a *shamisen*

Extra Activity

Ask students *Which do you think you would most like to go and see and why? Have you ever seen any theatre with puppets? Are there any traditional forms of theatre in your country?*

Exercise 13, page 95

Tell students that in order to talk about traditions you often need to refer to dates and periods of time in the past. In pairs, students complete the matching exercise. Students may find it easier to put the periods of history in order first and then match to the dates. Write the answers on the board for students to quickly check.

1 c 2 d 3 e 4 b 5 a 6 f

Exercise 14, page 95

Ask students what historical age / event the four dates represent (the French Revolution, the First World War, the Iron Age, the Middle Ages). Students listen and repeat the pronunciation of the dates. Point out that, while all previous four-number years have been pronounced in paired numbers, this has changed for the year 2000 (pronounced *two thousand*) and above (though it is likely to revert to the former system as the numbers become longer). Ask students questions relating to local history to elicit further examples.

Professional practice, page 95

Go through the phrases with the class, giving examples of how they are used. Point out the different use of

At this time, usually referring to a point in time, e.g. *At this time, Buddhism lost official support in Japan.*

During this time which might mean
– *for all the period of time* (emphasising duration)
– *on more than one occasion in the period of time*
– *at some point in the period of time*

Also

During this period has the same meanings as *During this time*

Throughout this period refers only to *for all the period of time* (emphasising from the beginning to the end).

Exercise 15, page 95

Ask students what they know about Japanese history. Refer *A* students to page 115. Students read the time line. Encourage them to use the pictures and the context to deduce the meaning of unknown words. Be prepared to explain / translate: *an eruption, to publish*. Check students understand *circa* means about. Give students a few minutes to think about how they are going to express their questions. With a less confident class, get students to prepare their questions in pairs. During the activity, monitor the pronunciation of dates.

Tips: During an information gap speaking activity, make sure that students cannot read their partner's information. One way to do this is to have the students sitting at a distance from each other. This has the added advantage of making monitoring easier.

In order to prepare a timeline for their own country, students may need supplementary information. This could be obtained from the internet. To search for a brief history of a country, go to a travel guide, e.g. www.travel.dk.com, www.lonelyplanet.com or www.roughguides.com, select the country and then 'history'. Once students have this information, get them to work in pairs or small groups and select 10–15 major events to include in their timeline. Pairs / Groups then compare and justify their decisions, adapting their ideas if they wish. Circulate and monitor, concentrating on the pronunciation of dates, appropriate vocabulary and the past tense / past passive. Point out that the historical information should be concise, as in the example of Japan, before students start the final copy of the timeline.

Travel guide project

Students include either the timeline or the summary or both in their project.

Exercise 16, page 96

Tell students they are going to listen to three people talking about public holidays in their country. Play the extracts one at a time, pausing after each extract for students to compare in pairs. Replay any parts that students have missed or misunderstood. Feed back as a class. Ask students if they have any public holidays of similar origins in their country, e.g. honouring people who have died in a war, honouring a national hero or a harvest festival.

1 **Poppy Day / Britain / 11 November:** after the First World War many of the battle fields were covered in poppies, so people wear them now to honour the people who died in the war
2 **Tiradentes Day / Brazil / 21 April:** to commemorate the death of one of Brazil's greatest heroes, Joaquim José da Silva Xavier, who, as well as being a travelling doctor and dentist, led a revolutionary movement against Portuguese rule at the end of the 18th century
3 **Thanksgiving / USA / the fourth Thursday of November:** to commemorate the first successful harvest for the settlers in 1621, an event the settlers celebrated themselves with a great feast to which they invited the local Indians

Exercise 17, page 96

In pairs, students discuss the question. This should be brief to avoid pre-empting the longer speaking activity, exercise 19.

Exercise 18, page 96

Focus students' attention on the picture and ask students to describe what they can see. What country do they think this is? Students read the questions. Set a time limit of two minutes for students to find the answers in the text. Students compare their answers in pairs. Monitor and only go over those answers which the students have found difficult. Be prepared to explain / translate: *verandah* (a platform attached to the side of a house with a roof and floor but no outside wall). Ask students if they had heard of this festival.

1 Diwali
2 The festival of lights.
3 Around the end of October and the beginning of November.
4 Throughout India and in Hindu communities in other parts of the world.
5 Small oil lamps (or, in urban areas, candles or neon lights) are lit and placed around the home, in courtyards, on verandahs, in gardens, on walls and roof-tops, families get together, children give each other sweets and fireworks are let off.
6 It has different meanings in different areas of the country but everywhere it signifies the renewal of life.

Extra Activity

Students find and underline in the text words and expressions which are generally useful when describing festivals and traditions, e.g. *well-known, it is celebrated throughout ..., it is held on ..., it is known as ...it is a time for ..., it is common to... .*

Exercise 19, page 97

Get students to copy the table into their notebooks so they have enough space. Give students a suggestion of how many festivals they should write about per category or in total (a total of six is probably enough before the language becomes repetitive). Refer students to the useful language in the Professional practice box. Set a time limit of about 15 minutes for students to complete the table. Circulate and monitor. Make sure both students are taking notes so that they can be separated for the presentations. Encourage students to use the related vocabulary expressions from the unit. Fast finishers can practise presenting their information with their partner. Depending on the size of your class, you may decide to have the students do their presentations in groups or in open class. Give the students who are listening to the presentations questions to consider and discuss at the end of each talk, e.g. *Did you learn anything you didn't know before? Which of these festivals is most important to you / your grandparents? Why? Which is most interesting for tourists? Why?*

Extra Activity

Alternatively, each pair prepares notes on one of the categories. Students could research the festivals in their category in more detail using the internet. To find information on the background of festivals, use a search engine, such as yahoo.com or excite.com, and search for the name of the festival. The class then forms groups of three, each student having prepared a different category. They explain their findings to each other, and take notes on the festivals that others researched. Round up with a discussion on what was the most interesting information they learnt.

Exercise 20, page 97

Students read the introduction and the email. Get the students to underline in the email what they need to include in their reply (a list of festivals, recommendations as to which we should offer our US customers, why the festival is important, who it will appeal to, why it will attract tourists). In pairs or small groups, students discuss and note their answers to these points. Ask students how they are going to present their ideas to Mr Foley: while it is possible to write a formal letter, the most appropriate style for the reply is a report. Ask students how they think a report might differ from a letter: it should have an introduction, a main body and a conclusion and be divided into sub-headings. Discuss as a class possible sub-headings, e.g. introduction, (name of festival), why it is important, who it will appeal to, why it will attract (US) tourists, recommendation / conclusion. Give students 15–20 minutes, working in pairs / groups to write their first draft. They then compare these with another pair / group. Write the following questions on the board for the students to discuss:

Does the report include all the information that was asked for?
Is the report appropriately organised?
Is there any information you would add?
Is there any inappropriate information?
Is the grammar and spelling accurate?

Circulate and monitor these evaluations. It may be useful to highlight particularly good examples of language or organisation and / or general weaknesses to the class. Students could write the final copy in class or for homework. Round off with a brief class discussion on which festival of their country attracts most tourists and why.

Special interest tours

Unit Notes

Exercise 1, page 98

Focus students' attention on the picture. Discuss the questions in open class. Use the pictures to elicit / teach *scuba diving, hiking, dog-handling*. Ask *Has anyone ever been on a special interest holiday? What type of people are attracted to this kind of holiday?*

painting, murder-mystery (usually in a country hotel over a weekend, all guests and some actors are involved in solving a 'murder'), golf, mountaineering, fishing, horse-riding, writing, health and beauty, music festivals, aromatherapy, wine, photography, bird-watching, battlefields, cooking, singing

Exercise 2, page 98

Check words: *whale, yoga, gourmet cooking* (high quality). The pronunciation of the following words may need particular attention: whale /weɪl/, yoga /ˈjəʊɡə/, gourmet /ˈɡʊəmeɪ/, hiking /ˈhaɪkɪŋ/. Students discuss the question in pairs.

Exercise 3, page 98

Point out the instruction to underline the words that led them to the answer. Set a time limit of two minutes for students to do the matching activity. Students compare their answers and key words in pairs. Feed back briefly on answers and key words.

a scuba diving (snorkelling, underwater)
b whale watching (ecology, naturalist, wildlife)
c yoga (breathing, relaxation)
d dog-handling (canine, pet)
e painting (artistic)

Exercise 4, page 98

Students read the questions. Point out that the answers are not necessarily in the text, but should be deduced from general knowledge. Students complete the exercise in pairs.

1 a **2** c **3** e **4** d **5** b

Extra Activity

In pairs, and using a monolingual dictionary to check meanings, students find in the texts useful vocabulary related to the five types of holiday. They can then add the words in exercise 5 to these lists.

Exercise 5, page 99

Explain that all the words relate to one of the five special interest holidays. Provide each pair with a monolingual dictionary and give them five minutes to match the words with the holidays. Fast finishers could add extra words to the lists. Feed back as a class. The pronunciation of the following words may need particular attention: species /ˈspiːʃiːz/, whistle /ˈwɪsəl/, obey /əʊˈbeɪ/, lead /liːd/.

a aqualung (air tank), wreck, diving
b reserve, endangered species, fauna and flora
c prayer, monk, monastery
d whistle, obey, lead
e palette, brush, oils

Workbook: Vocabulary, page 60, exercise 4.

Exercise 6, page 99

Check words: *exclusive* (expensive and not welcoming people who are thought to be socially unsuitable). Students predict the stressed sounds before listening to check. Students practise saying the words.

<u>pho</u>tograph pho<u>to</u>graphy archae<u>o</u>logy <u>at</u>mosphere
e<u>co</u>logy eco<u>lo</u>gical ex<u>clu</u>sive Hima<u>la</u>yas
<u>ha</u>bitats <u>ar</u>chitecture explo<u>ra</u>tion veget<u>ar</u>ian

---

Extra Activity

In pairs, students discuss what type of special interest holiday each of these words could be related to. Circulate and monitor pronunciation.

Exercise 7, page 99

Students discuss the question in pairs. If they don't have a special or unusual hobby, ask the students to think of one which might be of interest to other people.

Exercise 8, page 100

Tell students they are going to hear part of a radio programme where a travel writer gives travel advice. Ask *Are there radio programmes like this in your country? What sort of information might the caller be interested in?* There are four callers. Play the cassette / CD, pausing after each caller to allow students to compare their ideas in pairs, explaining what they heard. Feed back as a class.

> **1** gourmet cooking **2** football **3** whale watching
> **4** gardening

Exercise 9, page 100

In pairs, students complete the answers they know. Depending on the listening comprehension level of the class, you could either ask for a minimal answer, i.e. *who to contact*, or a more detailed answer, i.e. *what they offer, how to contact them.* Play the cassette again, pausing after each caller for students to compare in pairs. Replay any parts that students have missed or misunderstood. Feed back as a class.

Caller 1	*Where can you learn to do gourmet cooking?* Gourmet Adventure holidays, Amalfi coast, Italy, look at their internet site.
Caller 2	*How do I organise going to a home game of either Madrid or Barcelona?* Contact Fanfare, an agency which does packages including flights, hotel and tickets.
Caller 3	*Are there any whale-watching expeditions in Canada or British Columbia?* Contact the Ecosystems Research Foundation.
Caller 4	*Could you recommend overseas gardens to visit?* Contact Adderley Garden Tours for gardens in Europe or Delightful Garden Tours for outside Europe.

Extra Activity

- Students role-play one or more of the conversations. Encourage them to improvise using their answers to exercise 9 as prompts.
- Students refer to the tapescript, Students' Book page 143, to help prepare in note form their own dialogue between Janet Jones and a caller with a different special interest. Choose one or two pairs to act out their dialogues for the class.

Language focus, page 100

1 Tell students that the six example sentences are all from the listening. Ask students to identify who said each one: the host, Janet or a caller. Check students understand *less likely* means less probable. Check that students know that *'d* in sentence 4 represents *would*. Students match the examples and the uses. Feed back on these answers before moving on to part 2, which looks more closely at the forms of the sentences.

> **a** 1, 3, 6 **b** 4, 5 **c** 2

2 In pairs, students discuss whether the sentences are true or false, referring to the example sentences. Monitor their discussions and assess how much further clarification is necessary.

> **a** T
> **b** F *Will* is used in the main clause.
> **c** T
> **d** F The past is used to refer to an unreal / hypothetical present / future situation. It is the subjunctive in English. If students have a subjunctive in their own language / are familiar with this grammatical term, point this out to them.
> **e** T
> **f** T

3 Highlight that these types of sentences are a common way of giving advice. Go through the example sentences with the class. Use the first example to point out that, when referring to a less likely possibility, you can use *was* or *were* after *if I, he, she*. Give students a problem, e.g. *I feel ill*, and they offer advice using the structures.

> ### Extra Activity
> Students should be familiar with these forms but it is worth revising:
> – the contractions of *will* (*'ll*) and *would* (*'d*)
> – the negative of *will* (*won't*) and *would* (*wouldn't*)
> You may also decide to summarise the conditional forms:
>
> | | | |
> |---|---|---|
> | Zero conditional: | *if* + present | present |
> | First conditional: | *if* + present | *will, going to, can, must, may, should,* imperative |
> | Second conditional: | *if* + past | *would, might, could* |

Workbook: Conditionals, pages 60 and 61, exercises 5 and 6.

Exercise 10, page 101

Check words: *get arrested, be retired*. Encourage students to use a process of elimination to finish the exercise and deduce the meaning of further unknown words. Students work individually and then compare in pairs. Monitor the pronunciation of the contracted forms of *will* and *would*.

1 g 2 f 3 a 4 c 5 h 6 e 7 d 8 b

Exercise 11, page 101

Demonstrate this activity by asking the students a couple of questions. Get them to ask you some questions, too. If necessary, write the question head on the board: *Under what circumstances would you ... ?* Fast finishers can invent and discuss further questions.

Exercise 12, page 101

Check words: *honeymoon, folk music* (traditional in a community). Tell students they are going to role-play a conversation between a couple planning a honeymoon and a travel agent. Refer students to pages 101 and 117 of the Students' Book and allow ten minutes to prepare for the role-play.

Students *A* work together in small groups. They read the notes and underline what they want to be able to do and how much they want to spend on their holiday. They should check unknown vocabulary with each other. Get them to prepare four or five further questions that they could ask the travel agent, using conditional structures as much as possible.

Students *B* turn to page 117 and work together in small groups. They read the descriptions of the three holidays and check unknown vocabulary with each other / in a monolingual dictionary. To check comprehension, ask students to discuss the differences, advantages and disadvantages of the three holidays.

Pair *A* and *B* students together. For a more authentic feel, have the travel agent seated behind a 'desk'. Give students ten minutes for the conversation, starting from the customer sitting down and the travel agent asking *'How can I help you?'* to the customer deciding on the holiday. Fast finishers could extend the conversation to booking the holiday. Circulate and note down errors / useful language for analysis and correction later. Concentrate on the use of conditionals. Feed back briefly on which was the most popular choice and why.

Exercise 13, page 102

Focus students' attention on the pictures of Egypt. Ask students *Has anyone been to Egypt? What are the major attractions for tourists in Egypt?* Students read the introduction to confirm their ideas. Be prepared to

explain / translate: *to head for, a tourist magnet, the bank* (of a lake), *a felucca*. Students read the introduction to the listening. Warn students that the speakers change their minds about the itinerary during the conversation and so to listen to the whole section before writing their answers. Play the recording once, pausing after each day has been fully discussed for students to compare their ideas with a partner. Replay any sections where the students haven't heard the answer or have misunderstood.

Fact File

A *felucca* is an ancient Egyptian sailing boat. Nowadays they are used for short trips and longer cruises on the Nile.

1 morning: Giza pyramids
2 afternoon: Egyptian Museum and the Tutankhamun collection
3 coach to Temple of Ramses II and Temple of Hathor
4 afternoon: flight over Aswan Dam to see dam and unfinished obelisk
5 overnight on board ship at Aswan
6 morning: Visit to West Bank to see Valley of the Kings and Queens and the temple of Hatshepsut
7 afternoon: Relax before flight back
8 optional extra few days in Luxor with excursion to Karnak temples

Exercise 14, page 103

In pairs, students answer questions they already know. Repeat the listening, pausing as necessary for students to discuss their answers. Feedback as a class and ask the students *Would you be interested in this tour?*

1 The group will come out on a scheduled flight and stay in the Meridian Pyramids Hotel for two nights.
2 It's a lot to do in one day.
3 It's at 6 o'clock in the morning so the clients will have to get up at 2 am.
4 a short time / a morning.
5 It's more expensive as they will fly there.
6 2 nights – Tuesday and Wednesday.
7 A few days in Luxor with excursions to the Karnak complex.

> **Extra Activity**
>
> Students look through the tapescript, Students' Book page 143, and underline expressions of agreement and disagreement.

Professional practice, page 103

Tell students they are going to hold a similar discussion to the one they have just heard. Go through the phrases with the class. Explain what is meant by *soften the impact* (make the disagreement less direct).

Workbook; Agreeing and disagreeing, page 61, exercise 7.

Exercise 15, page 103

This activity works best, in terms of producing the language of agreement and disagreement, if the students are given a couple of minutes to study the map individually and consider the possibilities and then launch straight into the speaking. Before the discussion starts, remind students to use a range of phrases for agreeing and disagreeing. Organise the students into small groups of 3–4 students and set a five-minute time limit for them to plan their cruise. Circulate and monitor, concentrating on how students agree and disagree. At the end, ask one or two of the groups to describe their plan.

> **Extra Activity**
>
> - Pyramid discussion. Having decided on a plan, groups combine and are asked to agree on one plan between them in a time limit of three minutes. Continue combining groups until the whole class agrees on one plan.
> - Repeat a discussion from earlier in the book, for example unit 3 exercise 19. This would also be good vocabulary revision.

Exercise 16, page 104

Students read the introduction to the game. Check they understand the rules of the game. Check possible vocabulary problems in the questions: *to call in sick, blind, to bargain* (to discuss a price), *souq* (Egyptian market). Put the students into small groups. They can use coins, rings, etc. as counters. Clarify that when a student lands on a square, someone else from the group needs to act out the supporting role.

Groups which finish quickly could do the squares that no-one landed on or adapt the questions for a local hotel and answer them. Feed back at the end by briefly asking who won in each group.

> **Extra Activity**
>
> **Further revision ideas**
>
> **Vocabulary**
>
> 1 Pictionary. Put students in two teams. Show one student from each team the word you want to revise. That student draws a picture to represent it on the board and their team guesses. Continue, changing the student who draws. The winning team is the one that guesses the most correctly.
>
> 2 Odd one out. Students write lists of four words where three are related and one is different, e.g. *humid, warm, tram, chilly*. They exchange their lists with other pairs and identify the words that are different.
>
> 3 Back to the board. One student from each team turns their back to the board. The rest of the team faces this team member and the board. Write a word on the board. The team must define the word to their member. The first one to identify the word wins a point. Change the student who is guessing the word and continue.
>
> **Grammar**
>
> 1 Noughts and crosses. Draw a noughts and crosses grid on the board. Divide the class into two teams. In each square put a structure to be revised, e.g. *some, any, much, many, enough,* etc. Teams make sentences using the word in their chosen square. If correct, they win the square.
>
> 2 Betting game. Write ten sentences, some grammatically correct, others not. Give students a time limit to decide. Each team can bet a maximum of 20 euros on a sentence being correct or incorrect. If they are right they double their money, if they are wrong, they lose it. The winning team is the one with the most money at the end.
>
> 3 Translation. Use in a monolingual class if you are competent in the students' L1. Write ten sentences in English which include the structures you want to revise. Give five sentences to pair *A* and five to pair *B*. They translate their sentences into L1 and then give them to the other pair to translate back to English.
>
> 4 Team projects. Write a list of the grammar areas covered in the course on the board. Students identify the four or five most problematic areas. Divide the class into teams who then prepare a presentation on one of those areas. Students teach each other.

Consolidation 3

These exercises are designed to evaluate students' progress in assimilating the grammar and vocabulary from units 9–12. They are suitable for either revision or testing.

For revision purposes, review the language area with the students in open class first and then allow the students to work together in completing the exercises. Feed back as a class, asking for justification of the answer where appropriate.

For testing purposes, set a time limit for students to do one or more of the exercises individually in class. Alternatively, set the exercises as homework. Take the answers in to correct or provide the students with the answers to correct each other's.

You may also wish to evaluate students' progress in communicative performance. To do this, repeat one of the speaking / writing activities from the units. To increase the interest and challenge factors in this, change one or two features, e.g., students role-play a waiter and customers using a different menu.

Exercise 1, page 106

Review the rules on when to use the different quantifiers. Refer to the Language focus box on Students' Book page 87 and the Grammar reference section on page 128.

1 Ø **2** any **3** a few **4** Some **5** any **6** a little **7** Any
8 Few **9** some / a few **10** a few **11** Any **12** little

Exercise 2, page 106

Review the form of defining relative clauses. Refer to the Language focus box on Students' Book page 93 and the Grammar reference section on page 129. Explain to students that, in this exercise, it is more important that they get the form of the sentence right than the content.

Possible answers
2 Goulash is a meat stew that / which is originally from Hungary.
3 Sushi is rice with small pieces of food, normally raw fish, on top that / which is served in Japan.
4 Croissants are pastries that / which are eaten in France for breakfast.
5 Paella is a Spanish dish that / which consists of rice, vegetables, fish and chicken.
6 Blinis are pancakes that / which are served in Russia.
7 Gnochi are small round balls that / which are made of potato, wheat and water and that / which are usually served in soup or with a sauce.

Exercise 3, page 106

Review the form and use of conditionals. Refer to the Language focus box on Students' Book page 100 and the Grammar reference section on page 129.

1 b **2** a **3** e **4** g **5** h **6** f **7** c **8** d

Exercise 4, page 107

Refer to the vocabulary exercise on Students' Book page 86.

1 wine, water **2** fish, meat **3** grapes **4** tea, honey, jam
5 wine, water **6** bread, cake **7** parsley **8** lamb

Exercise 5, page 107

Students may have different answers from the following. Accept those which students can justify.

1 trek (the others are generally related to travelling by sea)
2 stay (the others can all be used to talk about taking transport)
3 overbooking (the others are all related to insurance)
4 roast (the others are all ways of cooking eggs)
5 poultry (the others are adjectives to describe food)
6 fireworks (the others are related to the theatre)
7 camera (the others are related to painting)
8 monastery (the others are all related to Egypt)

Exercise 6, page 107

Check students understand all the words. Provide an example for each stress pattern.

■ ■ ■ aqualung, atmosphere, habitats, photograph
■ ■ ■ artistic, endangered, exclusive, relaxing

Exercise 7, page 107

Demonstrate the six sounds and elicit example words first, e.g., ago /əgəʊ/, door /dɔː/, blue /bluː/, know /nəʊ/, now /naʊ/, up /ʌp/.

1 d **2** e **3** a **4** f **5** c **6** b

Unit 1: Choosing the best candidate

EDINBURGH CASTLE

Tour Guide Supervisor

Immediate full-time opening for Tour Guide Supervisor

Duties include organising daily tours, conducting tours and supervising tour guides. Must be clear and effective speaker, have strong interpersonal and organisational skills and enjoy working with the public.

Languages preferable.

Minimum 2 years' experience in the visitor industry.

Attractive salary.

A

Name: Steve Fielding
Age: 51
Nationality: British
Native language: English
Marital status: married, 2 children
Work experience:
now working as tourist information centre accounts manager
has worked in tourism industry for 20 years
Skills / interests:
accountancy qualifications
good computer skills
speaks a little French but hasn't used it in a long time
Interview notes:
- *friendly and enthusiastic, seems hard-working*
- *wants this job because wants more contact with people*
- *earns more in his current job than he could in this job*

B

Name: Sandrine Parnet
Age: 34
Nationality: French
Native language: French
Marital status: married
Work experience:
now working as public relations officer for multinational company
worked as a tour guide with groups of children from US travelling in Europe 10 years ago
Skills:
recently finished tourism course (Open University)
speaks English fluently, good Spanish and Italian
good computer skills
Interview notes:
- *wants to change jobs because she wants something more local that doesn't involve travelling*
- *calm and confident (a bit cold?)*

C

Name: Joe Schulz
Age: 25
Nationality: Swiss
Native language: German
Marital status: single
Work experience:
works as tour operator representative in skiing resort in Switzerland in winter
summer – supervises 10 teachers in a summer camp where students learn English and do sports
Skills:
high level of spoken English but low level of written English, some French
some computer skills
studied history at university, very interested in history
Interview notes:
- *very friendly and outgoing*
- *perhaps a bit informal?*
- *if offered job would move to Edinburgh*
- *excellent references*
- *available immediately*

Unit 2: Choosing a place to visit

Tourist information A

You have been asked to talk to a travel journalist about the attractions of Glasgow and how tourism is developing.

Sightseeing:

The Burrell Collection: housed in a spectacular museum, an eccentric collection of everything from Chinese porcelain and medieval furniture to paintings by Renoir and Cézanne.

Glasgow cathedral: wonderful Gothic architecture, most of the building is over 600 years old.

The Tenement House: an extraordinary time-capsule experience – a small apartment which shows how the middle class lived 100 years ago.

Paisley: town near Glasgow famous for its fabric design – museum with examples and history of the design.

Entertainment:

Lively nightlife

Celtic music festival in January

Arts and dance festival in May

International jazz festival in July

Food and drink:

Many pubs, wine bars, restaurants, traditional tearooms and coffee houses offering a wide range of cuisine: traditional Scottish (Scottish salmon, wood-smoked haddock, *haggis*), French, Indian, Mexican, Chinese, Italian and Thai.

Climate:

Cool temperate climate

Weather changes quickly – as some local people say 'If you don't like the weather, just wait five minutes.'

Driest months are May and June, but expect rain at any time.

Getting around:

Buses every 30 minutes from airport to city centre.

Roundabout ticket covers all underground and train transport in the city for a day (3-day version also available).

Tourist buses run every 20 minutes along main sightseeing routes.

How tourism is changing:

Always known for the friendliness of its inhabitants.

Previously associated with unemployment and economic depression.

Glasgow is reinventing itself, rediscovering its cultural roots – becoming more fashionable and attracting more tourists, opening new trendy bars and restaurants.

The UK's City of Architecture and Design in 1999.

Tourist information B

You have been asked to talk to a travel journalist about the attractions of Luxor and how tourism is developing.

Sightseeing:

Karnak temple – spectacular temple dedicated to the Theban gods, takes at least three hours to visit it.

Valley of the Kings – tombs of the pharaohs.

Temple of Hatshepsut – impressive temple of Queen Hatshepsut – dressed as a man and declared herself pharaoh, she ruled Egypt for 20 years.

Entertainment:

Sound and light show at Karnak temple – extravaganza that tells the history of Thebes and the lives of many of the pharaohs who built the temple.

Watch sunset from felucca (sailing boat).

Hot air balloon over the Valley of the Kings.

Food and drink:

Abundant Egyptian cuisine such as *felafel* (fried chickpeas and spices) and *kushari* (noodles, rice, lentils and onions in tomato sauce). Cheap, though not much variety available.

Climate:

Best to go Nov–March when temperatures are comfortable

Hot (over 35ºC) and dry April–Sept

Getting around:

No buses from the airport to the city, 7 km apart.

Easiest way to get round Luxor is by bicycle.

Hantour (horse and carriage) – need to agree price with driver.

Felucca for short trips around Luxor.

How tourism is changing:

Busy in cooler months.

Trying to attract more visitors in the summer by offering cheap package holidays with tours of the sights included.

Becoming very tourist-centred – difficult for tourists to walk around the city because of number of locals trying to sell products or encourage them to take a *hantour*.

Travel journalist

You have been asked to write an article about a tourist destination for young people. Ask the tourist information centre about Glasgow / Luxor and make a note of things that might interest young people.

Ask about:

- main attractions
- entertainment
- food and drink
- climate
- getting around
- how tourism is changing

Travel journalist

You have been asked to write an article about a tourist destination for young people. Ask the tourist information centre about Glasgow / Luxor and make a note of things that might interest young people.

Ask about:

- main attractions
- entertainment
- food and drink
- climate
- getting around
- how tourism is changing

Unit 3: Choosing a hotel

Student A

You are a tourist information agent. A tourist wants information about hotels in Berlin. Look at these three hotel descriptions and the notes you have made about them and answer his / her questions.

Hotel Unter den Linden

🛏 1 ⊞ 📺 ✉ ✈ ↗ ➤ P ☂
🍴 ⧉ *AE, DC, MC, V, JCB, EC.*
€€

This is the cheapest hotel in the area around Unter den Linden street, the most attractive area of Berlin, where many historic buildings and museums are located. It was one of the best hotels in the city but now the furniture is worn and the fittings are unreliable.

the hotel car park has limited space and is often full
some complaints about unfriendly service

DeragHotel Grosser Kurfürst

🛏 1 ⊞ 24 📺 ☂ ✉ 🍴 🛁 ✈
♿ ↗ ☂ 🍴 ⧉ *AE, DC, MC, V, EC.*
€€€

Opened in 1997, this is a middle-range hotel with modern facilities in a quiet location. It specialises in additional services for tourists. For example, the price of a room includes free public transport or bicycle hire.

30 minutes by public transport from city centre
hotel is next to an underground station

Hotel am Anhalter Bahnhof

1 📺 ☂ ✉ *MC, V, EC.*
€

This small and friendly hotel is situated in an old apartment block. Its low prices only apply to rooms without bathrooms. You pay more for rooms with a bath. The more expensive rooms face onto a courtyard and so are quieter, while the cheaper rooms overlook a busy street.

20 minutes from city centre
artistic, alternative area of Berlin – nightclubs, cinemas, theatres and galleries
public car park near hotel

> Price categories for a standard double room per night, including breakfast, tax and service:
> € under €100
> €€ €100–€150
> €€€ €150–€200
> €€€€ €200–€250
> €€€€€ more than–€250

Student B

You and three friends have just arrived in Berlin. You haven't booked a hotel room yet. You go to the tourist information centre to ask for recommendations about places to stay.

You are looking for a hotel which:

- is near Berlin's most well-known sights because you only have two days to visit Berlin
- is cheap (you don't have much money)
- has parking facilities (you are travelling by car)
- has rooms with a bathroom or shower
- is quiet (the last hotel you stayed in was big and noisy and you didn't sleep well)
- is modern and clean

Unit 4: A nightmare holiday

7 nights
in one of the
Caribbean's
most exclusive resorts
for just $860!

Stay in the luxurious Sunset Hotel, which offers you:

* rooms overlooking the ocean

* restaurant with local and international cuisine

* 2 bars including poolside BBQ bar

* outdoor swimming pool and spa

* beachside sports

* mountain bikes and jeep rental

* baby-sitting service

And our all-in-one price includes:

* collection from airport by hotel representative

* transport from the airport to the hotel

* organised excursions to local places of interest

* use of snorkelling mask and fins

Book now while the offer lasts!

Tourist role card

You, your wife / husband and your two-year-old daughter have just come back from this resort and it was the worst holiday of your life. You are going to complain to the tour operator and try to get some compensation. Here are some of the problems you had:

- You were not collected from airport. You had to pay $50 for a taxi to take you to the hotel.

- The room overlooked the swimming pool and bar. You only had a partial view of the ocean.

- The swimming pool was unsuitable for children: it was crowded and there was no lifeguard.

- The spa wasn't working.

- The local beaches were all private. The nearest public beach was a 20-minute walk from the hotel.

- The outside bar was open all night and very noisy. You and your family couldn't sleep.

- On two nights the restaurant only provided local food which your daughter couldn't eat.

- All the excursions were fully booked when you arrived.

Useful expressions

I want to complain about ...

A number of things went wrong. To start with ...

What's more ...

Another complaint I have is ...

Another problem we had was ...

I believe I am entitled to a refund.

Tour operator role card

You sell all-inclusive holidays to the Caribbean. You have had some complaints about the package holiday in the Sunset Hotel. You are going to talk to someone who has just returned from their holiday. Apologise and explain why things went wrong where possible. You can give him / her some compensation but not more than the equivalent of $250.

Here are some of the problems you know about:

- The hotel only has one bus for collecting guests from the hotel. If they cannot be at the airport exactly at the time the flight arrives, they expect the guest to wait at the airport.

- You have to pay a supplement for rooms which have a direct view of the ocean. Most of the rooms only have a partial view.

- The spa is currently closed for repair.

- The beach is a short distance from the hotel. The advertisement doesn't say that the hotel is near the beach.

- Last week was the local carnival so the bars were open all night.

- For the same reason, the restaurant decided to provide only local food for two of the nights.

- The excursions have been very popular recently because of the bad weather.

Useful expressions

What exactly was the problem?

I'm very sorry to hear that.

I can explain that. You see, ...

I'll make a note of that now and I'll look into it.

Thank you for bringing these matters to our attention.

In compensation I'd like to offer you ...

Unit 5: Dealing with a complaint

Student A

You are a guest at a hotel. This is the second time you have stayed here. Yesterday you arrived tired and late because your flight was delayed. The room you reserved had been given to another guest. The one you were given was smaller and noisier. You didn't sleep well. This morning you phoned room service three times to ask for breakfast in your room. In the end, you couldn't wait any longer and went down to the restaurant for breakfast. Now you are checking out and you notice on your bill that you have been charged extra for room service. Speak to the hotel manager about your dissatisfaction with the hotel service.

Useful expressions

I'm extremely dissatisfied with ...

I was(n't) told ...

I asked for ... but ...

What's more, when I ...

Can you tell me what you are going to do about this?

Student B

You are the hotel manager.

- If a flight arrives late it is not the responsibility of the hotel.

- If guests do not check in before 8 pm and do not inform the hotel it is quite normal for the hotel to let the room to another guest.

- If a guest is not satisfied with their room the management will do its best to provide a more suitable room.

- Two of the morning restaurant staff called in ill today.

- If a guest is unhappy with the hotel service, the management usually offer an appropriate compensation.

Useful expressions

Why don't we go through to my office?

The hotel has the right to ...

I'm extremely sorry about this / that.

I can explain why ...

I'll sort out this mistake.

I can assure you that ...

Unit 6: Futures game

1   I need to phone Mr Rownes at the Hotel Meridien but I haven't got the number.

Don't worry. I look it up.

2   Have you booked a hotel room for while you are in Madrid?

Yes, we're staying in the Hotel Regente for the two nights.

3   We've decided to go to Italy this year.

Really. I'm sure you'll love it. How will you get there?

4   How will you pay Mrs Gray?

By Visa.

5   Here are the tickets. The show is going to start at 8:30 pm. Would you like me to call a taxi for 8 pm?

Thank you. That'd be great.

6   Approximately what time will you be arriving?

The plane lands at 1:30 in the afternoon so we will probably arrive between 2 and 3 pm

7   The Jones family are going to join the cruise in Palma.

Are they? OK, I'm going to make a note of that.

8   Have you finalised all the arrangements with the tour operator?

Yes. We're signing the contract tomorrow.

9   Do you have the report on that resort you visited?

Not yet, I'm writing it up this afternoon.

10   How do we get to the hotel?

Don't worry about that. A representative from Sun Escapades Tours will be waiting for you when you arrive at the airport.

11   Your luggage will probably arrive on the next flight. Fill in this form and we are going to deliver it to your address tomorrow.

12   Did you know that Bici Tours will start several new cycling tours in southern France in June?

No, I didn't. Where did you read that?

Unit 9: Getting around Sydney

Plan A

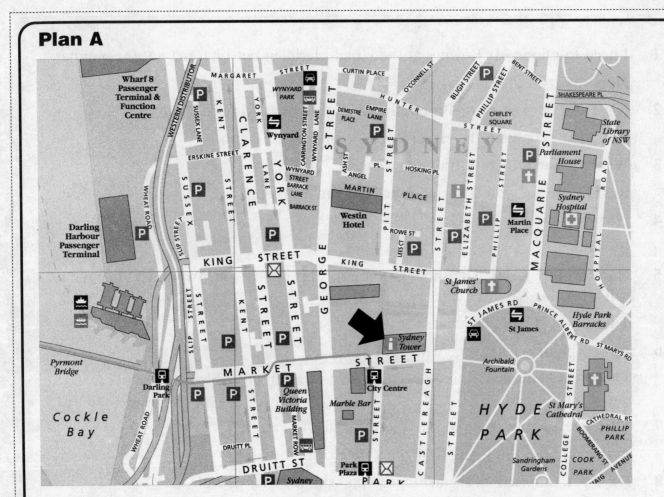

You are at the Tourist Information Office at Sydney Tower. Ask for directions to:

- *the nearest tourist information*
- *Westin Hotel*
- *St Mary's Cathedral*
- *Sydney Tower*
- *Sydney Hospital*

Mark the places on your map.

Respond to your partner's questions.

Useful expressions
Take the first / second / next street on the left / right.
Keep going until you come to / get to a / the ...
You'll see a / the ... on your left / right.
Go past the ...
Go left / right / straight on at the crossroads / traffic lights / junction.
It's on your left / right, next to / opposite / between ...

Plan B

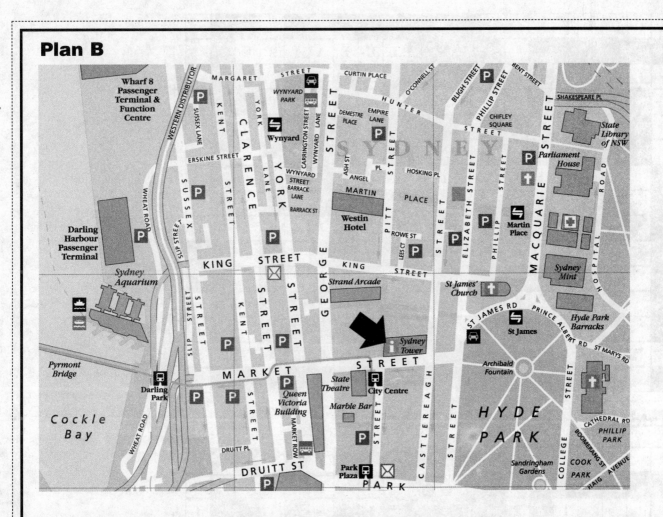

You are at the Tourist Infomation Office at Sydney Tower. Ask for directions to:

* *Strand Arcade*
* *State Library*
* *State Theatre*
* *Sydney Aquarium*
* *Sydney Mint*

Mark the places on your map.

Respond to your partner's questions.

Useful expressions
Take the first / second / next street on the left / right.
Keep going until you come to / get to a / the ...
You'll see a / the ... on your left / right.
Go past the ...
Go left / right / straight on at the crossroads / traffic lights / junction.
It's on your left / right, next to / opposite / between ...

Unit 11: Relative clauses crossword

Student A

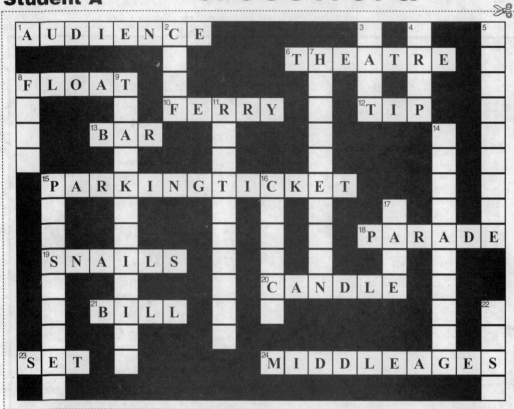

Student B

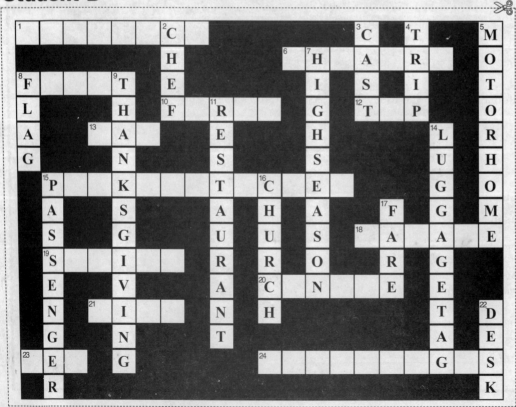